"Ready." She considered the word.

Ready indicated it was only a matter of time. Linus's words indicated that the time would never arrive. That was good, wasn't it? She didn't want the full truth, did she? She thought she didn't before...and now—

"Tough break."

Paula whirled to find Linus standing just a few feet behind her. His molten chocolate stare appeared more vibrant against the tropical morning sun as he, too, stared at the *Idella* disappearing around a bend in the bay.

"Guess they thought you wouldn't make it," he said.

"Wonder what would've given them that idea."

Linus barely shrugged in response. Paula rolled her eyes as she resumed her study of the quiet waters.

"If you're bummed about it," he said, moving closer, "I'm sure we could arrange something."

The offer made Paula smile. "I'm sure we could." She averted her face so he couldn't see her lashes flutter when he moved close to cup her hips.

"I'm not going to bed with you, L." She swallowed around the ball of need suddenly occupying her throat.

"That's the great thing about a place like this." He didn't seem discouraged by her decision. "There are all sorts of places we could substitute for a bed."

Dear Reader,

We're approaching the end of a long and wonderful road. I've been so fortunate to have you follow me on my journey with the cast of the Provocative series. I've enjoyed telling this story and introducing you to a group of Philadelphia powerhouses who joined forces to meet some pretty intense situations—the greatest among them falling in love.

I'm pleased to present Linus Brooks and Paula Starker in *Seductive Memory*. Much drama has settled in the worlds of these estranged lovers. Still, unspoken words and past regrets remain. To find the way back to the love they lost, Paula and Linus will have to shed their fears of facing the past and take hold of the desire still igniting between them.

I've enjoyed creating this world. Thank you for welcoming my stories and the characters who bring them to life.

Peace and Blessings Always,

AlTonya

altonya@lovealtonya.com

Seductive Memory

AlTonya Washington

HARLEQUIN® KIMANI™ ROMANCE

ISBN-13: 978-1-335-21686-1

Seductive Memory

For questions and comments about the quality of this book please contact us at CustomerService@Harlequin.com.

HARLEQUIN®
www.Harlequin.com

Printed in U.S.A.

AlTonya Washington has been a romance novelist for fifteen years. She's been nominated for numerous awards and is the winner of two RT Reviewers' Choice Best Book Awards for her novels *Finding Love Again* and *His Texas Touch*. She won the Romance Slam Jam EMMA Award for her novel *Indulge Me Tonight*. AlTonya lives in North Carolina and works as a reference librarian. This author wears many hats, but being a mom is her favorite job.

Books by AlTonya Washington

Harlequin Kimani Romance

As Good as the First Time
Every Chance I Get
Private Melody
Pleasure After Hours
Texas Love Song
His Texas Touch
Provocative Territory
Provocative Passion
Trust In Us
Indulge Me Tonight
Embrace My Heart
Treasure My Heart
Provocative Attraction
Silver Screen Romance
Seductive Memory

Visit the Author Profile page at Harlequin.com for more titles.

To my loyal readers, thank you for cheering me on.
Your support over the years has meant the world to me.

Prologue

Costalegre, Mexico

The wedding plans had changed, and quite suddenly. The bride and groom had opted for an event with a lot less flash and dazzle than the bride's mother would've liked. Still, no one could argue that the ceremony hadn't been a perfect one.

Santigo Rodriguez and Sophia Hail had spoken their romantic and heartfelt vows amid tropical breezes scented by the variety of exotic flowers adorning the environment. The change in venue and time had been a gift of sorts from the bride's sister and brother-in-law-to-be. Viva Hail and her fiancé, Rook Lourdess, had arranged a breathtaking escape that the bride and groom had eagerly accepted.

Flora of such splendid hues looked to have been skillfully shaded, as if from the colors of an artist's palette. The flowers, brilliant as they were, simply enhanced the sky. To call it magnificent just didn't seem to do it justice.

Paula Starker didn't think there were any words that could describe the presence of something capable of instilling such an intense sensation of serenity. And she could use a little serenity just then. The vivid blue, dotted by blindingly white and puffy clouds, infused her bloodstream with calmness like a drug. Paula was eager to let it have its way.

Serenity—as much as she could get—would remain a necessity if she was expected to make it through the rest of the day. She hadn't thought to ask Sophia how long a maid of honor was expected to hang around once the nuptials had concluded, especially when she had two. Viva had stood up with her sister as well.

Of course, such questions hadn't occurred to her until she'd realized who else she'd be sharing the ceremonial stage with. She'd actually been enjoying—or at least relatively enjoying—herself. The ceremony, its locale and the weather were all beautiful. Here were the good things of life—love, beauty, relaxation—all rolled into one. Who could ask for more?

Well, for starters, not having the man she almost married watching her throughout the entire occasion might've been nice. It should've been easy to ignore him. Seriously though, what woman with working eyes could truly ignore Linus Brooks? Especially when he stood just over thirty feet away? One of the groom's two best men, he epitomized tall, dark and stunning in linen trousers and a shirt as blindingly white as the clouds dotting the magnificent sky above.

He watched her with an unerring intensity that came across as just enough amusement and certainty. The look told Paula that he knew damn well the effect he was having on her. It didn't take a psychic to know the direction of her thoughts when her eyes lingered on his shirt billowing against the strong breeze.

Linus Brooks was well over six feet of taut, licorice muscle. His lean frame flattered every stitch of clothing he wore. This shirt was no different in the way it beautifully contrasted with his skin tone, and accentuated a sleekly sculpted chest.

Oh, he knew what he was doing, alright. Paula focused on keeping her brooding to a minimum, which helped to keep her eyes off the man who'd once held her body and soul in the palm of his hand. The heated reminder almost knocked the wind out of her. Surprising, since it was a truth never all that far from memory. Regardless, it was a truth that evoked a reaction when in the presence of the one it involved.

Linus Brooks had been that one—the only man she had ever wanted. Standing within sight of him then, Paula feared he always would be.

Costalegre's vibrant flowers and sky were rivaled strongly by its waters. Unending turquoise ran alongside the Pacific and had the ability to mesmerize onlookers with little effort. Paula was no exception. She had abandoned the lively beachfront reception not long after it had gotten underway. Though the sun was setting, it took nothing away from the brilliance of the day—in fact, it enhanced it. She'd already strolled along the shoreline, smiling as the water worked its way between her toes.

The maids of honor had been decked in linen, same as the best men. Sophia had selected baby doll dresses with capped sleeves and lace hems that were perfectly suited to the climate. The dress code forbade shoes, and Paula couldn't have been happier. She moved into the water until the tranquil waves lapped the backs of her knees. Serenity had found its way deep into her bloodstream, such that she wasn't *too* unsettled when his voice resonated above the quiet roar of the water.

"Some wedding," Linus noted while he too enjoyed the unending turquoise before his eyes.

"Some wedding," Paula managed, despite the violent stab of arousal his voice summoned.

"Tig and Sophie are already brainstorming ways to outdo this when they plan Rook and Viva's wedding."

Paula couldn't help but smile over the news Linus shared. "When couples compete, their friends get caught in the middle."

Linus grunted a laugh. "If the middle lands us here again, then I'm all for it."

"Yeah." Paula inhaled the pleasant air as she studied the sun making its way closer to the horizon.

"We should've been first."

His words clipped her appreciation of the view. "What?" She shifted to face him, gasping when her gaze collided with his. It had been years since she'd looked so closely into it. His eyes were molten chocolate orbs that had a sensually jarring glint and sometimes reflected hints of amber. His gaze was seductively set beneath long, thick brows of sleek ebony. Stricken, Paula directed her glare toward his pant legs rolled clear of the water.

"You heard me." Linus moved closer until he was taking Paula's other hand. Her fist was clenched tight near her thigh. "We should've been first. You should be my wife, have a house full of my kids and another inside you—"

"Linus, stop." She snatched her hand free and used it to cover her mouth. How long had it been since she'd spoken his name? "Don't." She hated the pleading quality she heard in her voice then.

"I'm sorry," he said.

The determined tone of his voice had Paula looking up again. She couldn't tell whether the apology spoke to their immediate conversation or to a situation long passed and best not revisited.

"It's too late," she said anyway. She couldn't resist probing to see whether their past was on his mind too.

It was.

"Is it?" He left barely a sliver of space between them then.

"It's a wedding, Linus. You're just getting caught up in the moment," Paula reasoned.

That was true. The moment was having its way with her as well. She wouldn't be able to resist leaning into him if he stayed where he was for much longer. Her thoughts buzzed with memories of the way he used to feel—strong, safe, capable of pleasure she'd never found a match for—

"Ma'am?"

Snapping to, Paula turned to give a nod to the tall dark-suited man who'd interrupted. He said nothing further, only turned and left once she'd acknowledged him.

"Was that for my benefit?" Linus asked.

Again, Paula smiled at the laughter in his query.

"No." She sighed. "I think we both know it'd take more than one member of my security team to have an effect on you. Anyway." She glanced across her shoulder to find that they were alone again on the quiet stretch of beach. "There's not much I can do without them, you know?"

Linus nodded. "One of the perks of being the district attorney," he said, only cringing a little at her dig.

"And one of the few I'll miss. He was just coming to let me know it's time," Paula explained before Linus could follow up his curious look with a question.

"That's why I came to find you." He nodded again, then said suddenly, as though remembering, "Sophie said you're on your way back to Philly."

"Yeah, um, they moved up the wedding date and threw me off schedule, so..." She shrugged. "Best I could do to make it work."

"But you just got here last night." A teasing light glimmered in his eyes. "Surely the DA can finagle a week off to celebrate her best friend's wedding?"

"There's a lot going on at the office." Paula issued the response she'd gotten down pat with all Sophie's begging for her to take more time as well. Truthfully speaking, it would've taken little more than her saying she'd be back when she got back if she'd wanted to "finagle" a week off or more.

She hadn't wanted it, and the reason was standing right beside her.

"You know, I never got to tell you how proud I am of you," Linus was saying, the pride he spoke of alive and well in his eyes. "You wanted DA and you got it."

"Not bad for an opportunist, huh?"

"Paula—"

"But that's not the word you used, was it?" She expected her words to have him stepping back.

Linus didn't budge. "May I talk to you?"

"About what, Linus? The past? The fact that we should've been first and I should be spending my time having your babies? We aren't them." She threw a hand toward the general direction of the beachfront reception. "Love? Future? We already know what that turns into, don't we?" She was the one stepping back then. "I already said my goodbyes." She turned to leave.

He blocked her way. "Don't you want to know why?"

"I did." Paula swallowed past a rising sob and silently celebrated the accomplishment. "I did when I was that heartbroken little girl, confused and shattered by the guy I would've killed for if he'd asked me to."

With a resigned shake of her head, she backed off a few more steps.

"I'm not the girl you knew, Linus. She's gone. You saw to that."

Chapter 1

Philadelphia, Pennsylvania
Three Weeks Later

"Maxton says the place will inspire our creativity." Elias Joss's piercing blue-green stare held a mix of doubt and curiosity as he observed the eight-by-eleven glossy in hand. The square work table before him carried several more of the aerial prints.

"Creativity, huh?" Santigo Rodriguez's gold-flecked dark gaze harbored similar doubt, which was laced with humor instead of curiosity. "Where's this villa he mentioned?"

Frowning slightly, Eli leaned over the table and upended another of the gold-toned folders that carried an additional sheaf of glossy images. "Here we go," he said.

Tig's light honey-toned face brightened with approval of the villa displayed in full color. It was tucked away on its own island a few miles from Finley Cay in The Bahamas.

"Now this is more like it," Tig breathed, as if awestruck. "Yeah… I could see myself getting very creative in there."

"Damn right." Eli's voice carried the same awe-filled chord. He had reached for one of the glossies as well and studied the immortalized image with distinct appreciation. "You thinkin' what I am?"

"I am, if you're thinkin' our work should be mixed with a few weeks of unadulterated playtime." Satisfied, Tig reclined in the wide ladder-backed chair to shuffle through a few more of the prints.

"Then it looks like our thoughts are one, my friend." Eli helped himself to a few prints from Tig's stack.

"I even have my playmate in mind." Tig's murmured words carried across the room.

"So do I," Eli murmured in return.

The snort that followed had both men looking toward the far end of the table.

"What?" Tig queried in reaction to the glare Linus sent his way.

"You're serious here?" Linus's expression reflected amused disbelief. "I could swear you just got back from two weeks of unadulterated playtime with your playmate."

"We're newlyweds, Line." Tig sighed matter-of-factly while giving a lazy stretch. "It's my duty as a husband to keep my wife in bed for the better part of the next two years at least."

"Good to know you take your vows seriously," Linus noted while Eli chuckled.

Again, Tig sighed. "It's an exhausting job, but I'll survive somehow."

Linus's quick grimace sent the hint of a dimple flashing in his cheek. "You know Maxton will expect us to get just a little work done?" he said.

"See? This is why you're their favorite."

"I'm everyone's favorite," Linus countered. "Without me, they don't get through the front door to the two of you."

"And here they are, already through the front door, and you're still their go-to guy because you keep us all on the straight and narrow."

It was true. Linus's outspoken nature and often biting wit had built him a respected name. Instead of clients shying away from his frequently intimidating persona, they appreciated the integrity that accompanied it.

"Line's right." Eli sobered. "Besides brainstorming ideas to turn this villa—and the island it sits on—into a worthwhile resort, we've got a stack of potential projects to decide on."

Expressions on the three handsome faces in the room grew distinctly downcast. The partners of Joss Construction eyed the rust-colored accordion folder they'd been avoiding. Secured by a rubber band, the folder was fat with potential groundbreakers.

Joss was among a very select few in the construction

business that rarely put in bids for jobs. The luxury of clients seeking them out for first refusals was one they'd worked very hard to acquire. Linus, Elias and Santigo had already taken preliminary meetings concerning each proposal. They had yet to decide which ones to add to an already robust lineup. Of course, being busy was nothing new for the talented trio.

Joss Construction was Elias's inheritance, but his friends shared equally in the partnership. The three—friends since before they could talk—had taken Evan Joss's brainchild and carried it to even greater heights of success and respect. While Elias believed that his late father would've never admitted he'd been surpassed in the business, he knew the man could never have argued it as fact.

Still, despite the partners' notable accomplishments, clients who offered tropical escapes to exclusive, fully furnished villas on private islands in The Bahamas didn't come around every day.

"Is it just me or does it seem like Line isn't comprehending all the fringe benefits of this getaway?"

"He's just stressing over which of his many playmates to bring."

Tig laughed over Eli's remark. "Not to worry, Line. According to the list of amenities, the place is segmented into ten suites. You can bring at least two of your playmates."

"At least," Eli agreed.

"We can't forget Bark though. He'll need a place to tuck away one of his guests." Tig referred to another close friend from the before-they-could-talk stage, Barker Grant.

"Bark isn't all that showy." Eli smirked. "Most likely he'll be content with just one playmate. Line's in a whole different league."

"Hell yeah, he is." Tig smiled, nodding. "Alright, Line, if B's good with one guest, you can bring upwards of four lucky beauties. Tucked away in their own suites, everyone should be happy."

Eli grinned, and it seemed as though full-blown laughter would soon follow. Linus muttered an obscenity as he pushed back from the table. The movement diffused the good vibes circulating the room. Linus left without another word. The door slamming at his back sent frowns passing between his friends.

"Something I said?" Tig queried.

Eli shook his head, gaze still fixed on the conference room door. "No different than usual. We always give him grief about all the women he juggles."

"Yeah." Tig set aside the villa photos, having lost interest in them. "Guess there comes a time when a joke's been told too many times."

"Mmm… I don't think that's it though." Eli's gaze was still on the door. "Line's seemed…off for a while now. I noticed it when we got back from Cortina for your wedding."

"From Rook's place?" Tig referenced the home their friend kept in the small Italian province. "Think we should talk to him?" Tig shrugged at the skeptical look he got in return.

"You really want to do that while his temper is up?" Eli mused.

"Right." Tig wagged a finger in the air. "We'll wait 'til he's cooler."

Both men were well aware that a temper surge from Linus Brooks could be akin to setting a lit match to gasoline. They knew the man had made great strides in controlling the darkness when it took hold. They were also smart enough to know better than to tempt fate.

"Right," Elias said in response to Tig's suggestion. "We'll wait."

Boston, Massachusetts

Caught up in the moment. That's all it'd been. That's all it could ever be.

Paula Starker massaged her temples and then drew her fingers through the plump dark ringlets that covered her head in a flirty bob. Silently, she ordered the words to take hold of her psyche and convince her of their truth.

Linus had just been caught up in the moment; that's where all his…insane talk had come from. She began to tap her fingers to her forehead to convince the idea to take root. She couldn't quite make it stick, and knew the girl inside her was to blame. That was what happened when a woman went to war with the girl she'd been.

Paula had been sensing that girl—her former self—creeping closer to the surface of her consciousness ever since she'd seen Linus at the hospital following Sophie's accident during her investigation of a previous case. All it had taken was a look from him to have the girl clamoring back to the surface. When he'd taken her hand to shake it, the girl had nearly swooned.

Paula couldn't begrudge the girl her desires. More than anything, she wanted to give in to them too. The woman in her though…the woman was who she was now. Back then, the woman had swept in heroically to save the girl from being consumed by waves of self-pity. While the girl had only cared about being back in the arms of Linus Brooks, the woman had wanted to know why Linus Brooks had crushed her heart and left it to rot.

"Stop!" Paula gave a violent shake of her head. She was making too much of this now. Besides, she'd pretty much set him straight before storming off that beach in Mexico anyway.

The woman wanted answers, but she was also just fine with keeping things as they were. Yes, she deserved answers about the night things had changed between them so long ago. If she got them though…if she got them and her heart melted for him again… Paula knew neither the girl nor the woman would survive that kind of hurt twice in a lifetime.

Resting her head against the seat back, Paula studied the house at the top of the long winding brick drive.

"Hope you've got some words of wisdom, Professor B." She sighed and rolled her window down to speak into the callbox outside the iron gates securing the home of Dr. Miranda Bormann, Esquire. Paula's former professor and mentor had been her go-to source for answers to life's most perplexing questions.

Paula sure hoped the woman hadn't lost her knack for issuing excellent advice.

She ascended the wide front steps with more confidence than appreciation. Paula knew her confidence was most likely due to the fact that Miranda Bormann had been the one to reach out to request a visit. While Paula had kept healthy contact with her favorite professor over the years, she was usually the one to connect with offers to get together for dinner or a quick chat over afternoon tea, or coffee as it were.

She smiled, flexing her fingers around the handle of the paper bag she carried. The package contained a tin of Bormann's favorite French roast. As district attorney of a major city, it had been difficult for Paula to keep to a consistent schedule of visits, but she made a tremendous effort.

It was nice to be visiting by Bormann's invitation, rather than by her own request. Still, the technicalities didn't change the fact that Paula was in need of serious mentoring just then. Her troubled past and recent encounter with Linus Brooks weren't the only things wreaking havoc on her mind now.

Paula was poised to ring the bell when the broad pine door opened before her. She laughed, surprised and delighted to be met by the hostess herself.

Miranda Bormann personified what it meant to retire well. One reason was because the woman considered herself a lifelong student. She'd taken to acquiring firsthand knowledge of the world around her once she'd resigned from her tenure as a renowned law professor.

The various LISTSERVs and web groups Paula subscribed to often reported on what hidden corner of the world Bormann had travelled to.

Understated elegance was thc phrase that often followed a mention of Miranda Bormann's name. Her papers and lectures also graced the shelves of some of the finest libraries in the world.

Bormann, however, was no diva. She was happy whether she was speaking over commencement exercises at a major university or working tirelessly in her greenhouse or outdoor flower garden. When the woman answered the door now, it was obvious she'd been getting her hands dirty.

"Looks like I'm dressed for work." Paula spread her hands to indicate her worn jeans, sneakers and the lightweight sweatshirt under her jacket.

"For a change," Miranda Bormann scoffed, but her sky-blue eyes were sparkling playfully as she assessed the younger woman's attire. "It's usually Prada or Gucci with you. Get in here." Bormann pulled Paula into a tight embrace, which was followed by a cheek kiss.

"You always said clothes make the woman," Paula noted when they pulled apart and she presented Bormann with the coffee.

"Ooh!" the noted professor cooed. She sniffed inside the bag as though the aroma of the freshly ground beans was wafting from the can.

"Nooo," she said, her freckled nose scrunching in disagreement to Paula's words. "I said *perfectly pressed* clothes make the woman. Invest in a good iron, and folks won't know whether you're in Coco Chanel or

JC Penney. Now let's see if this tastes as good as it smells." Bormann hugged the bag close and led the way from the foyer.

"I was surprised to get your call," Paula said as she followed. "*I'm* usually the one bugging *you* for a visit."

"You never bug me! You keep me spry!" Bormann declared as she took the long corridor to her kitchen at a speed that had Paula sprinting to keep up.

"Glad to hear that."

Bormann's quick steps slowed, and she turned to eye Paula speculatively. "What's that tone?"

Paula shrugged. "Life stuff."

The playful sparkle in Bormann's eyes turned sly. "A young man?"

Paula laughed. "We aren't so young anymore."

Bormann stuck out her tongue. "You're a baby. Hank and I broke up four times before we were married and made a go of it for fifty-two years." She raised thin, perfectly arched brows.

Again, Paula laughed. "It's complicated."

"It always is, my love." Bormann turned and continued her trek down the corridor. "So…young man troubles and? Anything more to go on the day's agenda?" She breezed into the airy kitchen that looked to be half the size of a football field.

Paula took her place on one of the cushioned high-back stools dotting the long wood-grained island that separated the cooking space from a cozy breakfast nook and sunken den area. "The rest is about work."

"New case?" Bormann asked while scanning the labeling on the coffee tin.

"No." Paula focused on the invisible design she traced into the island top. "And I'm thinking about keeping it that way."

Bormann looked every bit the hard-nosed professor then as she eyed her former student. She set down the coffee tin and moved closer to Paula at the island. "Keeping it that way as District Attorney Paula Starker, or Paula Starker, Esquire?"

"I'm pretty sure District Attorney Paula Starker is history." Paula slumped against the stool back. "I'm not running for reelection. As for Paula Starker, Esquire… I'm not sure yet."

"That last case really got to you," Bormann noted, and began toying with the end of her dark braided ponytail.

"In a pretty big way." Paula saw no point in denying it.

There was no need to provide details. Paula's last case had made front page headlines nationwide. The inner workings of the Philadelphia Police Department had been a hot topic for months following the news of a money laundering scandal that had brought down several members of the department.

"It's not easy to prosecute cops you've worked with. I've bought Christmas presents for some of their kids and—" Paula couldn't continue. Her thoughts went to top members of the brass and even police academy instructors.

"I almost lost my best friend in the mix," she added, thinking of Chief of Detectives Sophia Hail-Rodriguez, who'd been targeted when she'd gotten too close to the truth. “That one hit way too close to home.” She shuddered while shaking her head. “I’ve had enough, Professor B. I mean I—I still love the law. I… I just don’t know what my place is in it anymore.”

“And how does your young man fit into this?”

“He doesn’t.”

Bormann smiled when Paula snapped the words.

Paula silently ordered herself to take it down a notch. “He’s a whole other pile of crap-drama, I mean.”

“Ah! So there’s love there.”

Paula looked confused. “Well, I just called him a pile of crap, so…”

Bormann seemed tickled. Clasping her hands, she grabbed the tin and turned for her coffeemaker. “We’ll discuss him first before we get to the real shitty part of the agenda.”

Paula noticed the woman was carrying a folder once she’d put the coffee on and turned back to the island.

“Before we talk about him, I’ve got no real advice to give about your political decisions other than to list all the pros and cons, weigh them dispassionately before you choose.” Bormann slid the folder across the woodgrain countertop to Paula.

“I can’t imagine what all it must take to be a DA,” she continued. “There are aspects to that job that can affect your decisions in ways I’m not capable of anticipating. As for your law career, I can tell you that there are all kinds of ways to serve. Maybe you need to find a new way.”

Paula glanced at the folder and smiled. “Will I find a way in there?”

Bormann shrugged. “Maybe a career in private practice could be your calling. If so, consider that—” she tapped the folder “—my request to become your first client.”

Paula’s smile vanished when her jaw dropped.

Chapter 2

He should've waited. He should've waited before pressing her to talk or to let him talk—explain. He *had* pressed though, and what had that gotten him except her telling him where to go? She'd reminded him with scalding efficiency of just how much he'd hurt her.

Now, three weeks later, that moment still maintained prime position in his head. She'd pretty much told him he had no chance with her, and yet he'd spent the better part of his time since the ill-fated encounter on the beach assuring himself that this wasn't over.

He couldn't fathom why he was so sure of that now, when they'd been out of each other's lives for ages. Linus knew why, of course. Paula had never been out of his head. Not really. Such a thing wasn't possible when she was the district attorney in the city he lived in.

Paula Starker was a frequent presence on his TV screen when a new case required her input for the evening broadcast. Not only that, but as a public figure—a beautiful public figure—her private life was also prime fodder for the rumor mill.

Linus could've done without all the buzz on the latest athlcte, actor or musician she'd been seen on the town with. Still, when the odd occasion arose where they wound up at the same event, he managed to make himself scarce. He made himself scarce when what he really wanted was to rip out the intestines of the latest idiot who thought to claim what was his. What *used to be* his, he reminded himself.

Such torture, however, didn't stop him from tuning in for the gossip. The celebrity involvements rarely lasted beyond a date or two. When she'd been caught out with someone he didn't recognize and those outings numbered beyond four...those were the times his heart seized in his chest. Those were the times he feared she was lost to him for good.

The fact that she wasn't lost to him for good gave him hope. Seeing her on that beach, though...witnessing the sheen of tears in her eyes not spilled...

He'd hurt her in the past, badly. Regardless of how much he assured himself that all wasn't hopeless between them now, there was no going forward until he told her why. He'd lost it that night, demolished the place that was meant to signify a defining moment in their futures. It was the place he'd planned to ask her to be his wife.

Linus sensed a numbness along his forearm and saw

that his drawn fist was to blame. He had long since triumphed over the anger—the rage—that had ruled him. There were times, however, when he believed he hadn't triumphed at all—that the demons had only lain in wait for the perfect thing to destroy.

It had been that way when he'd found Paula. He'd gone years without an episode, even joined his best friends on a completely bold venture to revamp an already successful and revered company. Linus had been the outspoken visionary behind Joss Construction when he met the ambitious new lawyer with future designs on turning the Philly political scene on its ear by becoming the city's first black female DA.

Life had been good then, and their chemistry had been explosive. Now, Linus's appetite for women had little to do with conquests and more to do with hope. It was the hope that a woman out there could make him forget Paula Starker. He didn't think such a woman existed. Their emotions had delved far beneath the shallow physical allure to collide with something far more powerful. The surface attraction, however, had done a total number on him. The confident lawyer with the nonstop curves had had him cold.

Linus had wanted Paula in the most desperate way, but he'd wanted more than the delights her body promised. He'd sensed a kinship—a connection of the spirit that surpassed the physical—and he had wanted to see where things could go between them. Such was not to be, and the blame for that rested right at his feet. He wanted—needed—to make it right. More than that, he wanted her back, wanted her to be his, the way she always should've been. His and his alone.

But what of the demons? The demons had waited ever so patiently to unleash their havoc-wreaking frenzy until he had been literally days away from securing a future with Paula. Giving her an explanation for that night and then just walking away wasn't an option for him. Neither was hurting her again.

Besides that, giving her an explanation—the one she deserved—meant revisiting a place he had sworn he was done with. A place that made him feel like nothing more than the scared kid he'd been instead of the accomplished man he'd become.

There was a sound on his office door that barely passed for a knock. Linus turned to see his partners hovering just past the threshold. Their wary expressions brought a much-needed smile to his face. Despite the smile, he had to wave them in before they moved any farther beyond the doorway.

"Este says you've been in here all afternoon." Tig referred to Linus's assistant, Estella Mays.

"Yeah," was Linus's only confirmation.

Tig looked helplessly to Eli, and both men appeared to be holding out little hope that their friend's mood had improved.

"So how'd the rest of the meeting go?"

Linus's query seemed to be the olive branch Tig and Eli needed. Noticeably more comfortable, they moved a little farther into the office.

"All went well. Everything seems in order," Tig said.

"Any pop in here, Line?" Eli asked on his way to the mini fridge.

"Yeah, help yourself."

Eli gave a nod and sent Tig a sly look across his shoulder.

"So it looks like Maxton's cool with us taking as much time as we need at the villa." Tig moved into the roomy living area that occupied over a third of the office space.

"Sounds good," Linus said, joining him.

"Me and E were thinkin', since we've got so much work to do with going over the rest of the proposals, it might be a good idea to just keep this strictly a business trip."

"Right." Linus settled into his preferred recliner. The smile curving his mouth gave away the fact that he was all too aware what had prompted the change in plans. Still, he pretended to be confused. "What about playtime with playthings?"

Tig cast aside the idea with a wave. "Sophie's already taken three weeks of her eight-week leave. Best to save the rest for when we come up with our master getaway to pay back Rook and Veev for Mexico."

"Mmm-hmm, and what about Clarissa?" Linus asked Eli, who was on his way to the living room with three bottles of soda in tow.

Eli smiled at the mention of his girlfriend, Clarissa David. "She's already feeling guilty for leaving Ray with so much of the workload—first the getaway to Cortina and then Mexico for Tig and Sophie's wedding. She's trying to get the woman to take some time for herself." Eli referred to Rayelle Keats. In addition to being Clarissa's best friend, Ray served as general manager for her late aunt's franchise of gentleman's clubs that were transitioning into dance studios.

"Trust us, it won't be all work," Tig said. "We'll take Rook and Bark along. Since Rook's new job keeps him up to his ears in snow for most of the year *and* if the weather guys get it right, we'll be getting our fill of it in a few weeks, so I don't think it'll be hard to convince Barker. We could make it a guys' getaway—hell, we're entitled to those, same as the girls," he added.

"Sure we are." Linus gave a half shrug. "Thing is, guys' getaways are a lot more fun when girls participate. No offence, but Rook and Bark aren't exactly the playmates who'd put that fun in motion."

"Yeah, well, it wouldn't be much fun if everybody didn't have a playmate," Tig observed.

Linus grinned, the gesture sparking his faint dimple. "You know, I won't have trouble finding one of those to bring along."

"Mmm, but not the one you want." Eli held his bottle poised for drinking while regarding his friend with quiet amusement. "Who is she?" he asked.

Linus's grin remained, but the gesture appeared just a tad forced. "Do you really need me to talk about my list of conquests now?"

"No. Just the one who's got you in this mood."

The grin vanished. In its place was a series of muscle twitches along the jawline. Linus left his recliner and began to pace the living area.

"We don't mean to pry, man." Tig winced. "If you don't want to talk—"

"It's okay." Linus shook his head. "I should've told you guys about her a long time ago."

"Girl from your past?" Tig guessed.

"*Way* past," Linus confirmed.

"We know her?" Eli asked.

"Yeah." Linus turned then, folding his arms over his chest while he leaned against a wall. "Paula Starker."

Tig and Eli exchanged looks.

"Paula?" Tig blurted.

"*DA* Paula Starker?" Eli emphasized.

Linus's lazy grin returned. "Yes and yes."

"Get the hell out of here!" Tig ordered, after silence had held the room in its grip for half a minute.

Eli roared with laughter. "Damn, man, if you didn't want to talk about it, you could've said so!"

"It's not a joke," Linus insisted, though he fully understood his friends' disbelief.

"She's the DA." Tig apparently felt the need to reiterate that fact.

Linus only smiled. "She wasn't always."

"How is this possible?" Eli wanted to know. "We've been friends since the crib."

Linus laughed heartily then. "Does that mean we have to know everything about each other?"

Eli shrugged. "I'd say everything else pales in comparison once you know someone crapped their pants up through first grade."

Laughter exploded between the old friends.

"Lies!" Linus roared. "That only happened when they served that green pudding for lunch."

"I gotta agree with E, man." Tig's tone brought a touch of seriousness back to the conversation. "Soph and Paula are best friends. She'd have mentioned it."

Linus grew more serious then too. "Guess she's done as good a job keeping it from her friends as I have from mine."

Eli leaned over to set his bottle on an end table. "What happened?" he asked.

"Lost my temper." Linus knew it wouldn't take much more than those words to give his friends a good idea of how things had derailed. Questions remained, however.

"Did you hit her?" The gold flecks in Tig's dark eyes glinted with unspoken disapproval.

"No." Self-disgust had sent the faint amber hue of Linus's gaze diluting to its molten chocolate state. "But I didn't much care where the furniture landed when I threw it. She wasn't touched, but she could've been." Linus reclaimed his seat on the recliner. "Touched or not, she got hurt just the same. I said things...called her names."

"What names?"

"The bad kind." Linus sent Eli a humorless smirk. "She's got every right to hate me, and she's made it clear that she does over the few times we've seen each other lately."

"In Cortina?" Eli shifted a meaningful look at Tig while referring to the recent trip they had taken to Rook Lourdess's home.

"Hmph, yeah." Linus shook his head in spite of himself. "Then there was Mexico."

Tig winced. "So I guess all the love and adoration that's been goin' around has been hell on you."

"You've got no idea, T." Linus managed a weary grin. "She should have been my wife by now. The night I lost it, I was gonna propose."

"Jesus, Line..." A measure of Eli's own temper surfaced then. "It was that serious and you never told us?"

"Nothin' personal, E." Linus shrugged weakly. "It was just so good for so long between us and I didn't want to do anything to set them off."

"Them?"

"My demons," Linus said in reply to Tig's query. "They'd been quiet for so long before that night. I thought maybe...maybe they were gone. That somehow I'd defeated them. It took that night to see there was no defeat, no triumph 'til I turned and faced them."

"Looks like you have." Tig spread his hands in an encompassing gesture. "We haven't been witness to any furniture-throwing outbreaks lately."

"Paula hasn't been in my life lately, T. Sometimes I think all my so-called progress is a joke. It won't be real until I turn and face her—apologize for what I did."

"So what happened that night?" Eli queried, his expression a tad guarded. "To make you do what you did?"

"That's not the point." Linus's features visibly sharpened as well. "The point is I did it and I need her to give me the chance to tell her how sorry I am."

The looks exchanged between Eli and Tig were laced with uncertainty again.

"An apology for what you did might go over better if you tell her why you did it," Tig noted.

Linus's features remained set. "Why doesn't matter."

"It might to her," Tig challenged.

Linus leaned forward then and held his head in his hands. Silently, he agreed.

"But that's for later. First, I want to hear about this young man."

Paula sent strongly worded mental orders to her brain to pick her jaw up off the ground. She watched Miranda Bormann with a mix of humor and disbelief.

"You can't just lay something like this on me and expect us to go back to talking about my love life," she said.

"Ah, so you *are* in love with him?"

"Professor B—"

"Humor an old woman, love."

"Okay. Where is she?" Paula countered.

Miranda Bormann's gaze sparkled slyly. "Nice try, but flattery won't help. I want to know about your young man. Let's start with when you met him."

"Alright." Paula anticipated the woman's surprise at what she would say next. "A few weeks before I got my law degree."

Miranda Bormann was indeed stunned. "You met him then, but I've never seen you with a diamond on a certain finger. What gives?"

"Remember that drama I spoke of? There was a ton of it."

Bormann blinked. "Still?"

The inquiry had Paula wincing. "It kind of carried over—it was hard to run from."

"Such are the ways things tend to be when it comes to drama with the one we love, and don't try telling me you're not in love with him. If you could see your face, you'd know that's what's written all over it."

"I can't let myself get snagged back into it, Professor B." Paula drew a hand through her loose curls. "I've come too far. I'm not the little idiot he knew."

"But he's still on your mind?"

"We've got mutual friends. We bump into each other sometimes since they've gotten back together." Paula tapped her fingers against the glossy countertop. "It keeps bringing all the other stuff back."

"And you can't ignore it?"

"Oh, I could." Paula swore and pushed away from the island to pace the kitchen. "But he wants to—to talk about it. To explain what went wrong."

"And you don't want to know."

"I want to know, but I—" Paula bowed her head, pressing her lips together as though she were trying to tell herself to get it together. "If he tells me what happened, I—I'm afraid I'll..."

"Fall deeper for him than you already have."

Paula looked directly at her mentor. "I can't let that happen."

"But, honey, why? Especially when it seems you both still have feelings for each other."

"Linus Brooks is a part of my past." Paula looked a mite flustered. "It's best he stays there."

"Linus Brooks." Something sharpened in Miranda Bormann's expression.

"I've done a pretty good job of not letting my heart have a say in any of this." Paula took no notice of Bormann's manner. "I've been pretty happy because of that. Guess I owe that to Linus. Dammit." Again, she tugged her fingers through her hair. "Why the hell does he have to come messing with my head now?"

Bormann stood. "You're a smart girl. I'm sure you'll figure out the best way to handle it." Bormann fidgeted with the ends of the braided ponytail she sported. Her dark hair was just beginning to show silver strands along her temples.

"Yeah, well…my head doesn't work so well with him inside it," Paula went on.

Bormann smiled. "It may not be such a bad idea to let your heart do a little talking either."

Paula snorted. "Please tell me it's time to change the subject."

"Are you sure you want that?"

Paula threw back her head. "More than sure!"

Miranda Bormann's smile looked defiant. "Just remember you said that."

The woman's tone had Paula eyeing her curiously. "What is it? What's really going on with you, Professor B?"

Bormann retrieved the folder from the island. She offered it to Paula.

"I'm guessing this is why you really wanted to see me?" Paula took the folder.

Bormann shrugged. “Of course not. You know I always enjoy our chats.”

“But?”

“But I need another perspective on this.”

“What is it?” Paula asked even as she flipped through the folder.

“I’ve always taught my students that it’s better to be armed with a cache of facts before charging in with allegations.” Bormann’s unreadable gaze was set on the folder. “Those are my facts—what little I’ve been able to gather.”

Paula closed the folder and joined Bormann, pulling the woman along with her to the den area across from the kitchen. “Talk to me, Professor,” she insisted once they were seated.

Bormann laughed quietly. “It’s my own damn fault for digging up a mess I’d probably have been able to live my life blissfully unaware of.”

The renowned lawyer aimed an index finger at her former pupil. “Don’t let anyone tell you different, Miss DA—retirement is a wonderful drug, but boredom is one bitch of a side effect.”

“What’d you find?” Paula asked through a tight smile.

“I married into all this.” Bormann raised her hands toward the high ceilings. “I married into Hank’s money, and he wasn’t any more interested in it than I was.” She smiled at the mention of her late husband, Henry Bormann.

“Still.” She sighed. “The money management fell to him as the firstborn. When he died, he’d made arrangements so I wouldn't have to deal with any of that. Most of my financial advisors are his family—the others are friends of the family."

"You don't trust them," Paula detected.

"I don't know who to trust. Which is why I've had an old friend from law school helping me on the sly, when my digging around uncovered some discrepancies I didn't expect."

"Discrepancies?"

"Oh, nothing's been taken," Bormann was quick to assure, "but I've noticed funds have…shifted on dates that coincided with times I've been away on speaking engagements. I wouldn't have been involved with moving funds then. I haven't come across anything that's been removed and not replaced, but Hank had a lot of private property outside of the family holdings. My friend confirmed that some of those properties have been earmarked for development."

Paula returned to shuffling through the folder. "Have you visited any of these sites?"

"Some, I'm sure. My husband's holdings were vast. There's no way of knowing which developments are on the up-and-up and which aren't." She gave an exasperated huff. "Maybe they *are* on the level, and it's just the shifting of funds that has me suspicious. Regardless, I can't go to any of the family with this."

"Why's that?"

Bormann's exasperation mixed with frustration. "For one, my nephew has immediate control of my assets and I'd rather not alert him until I have enough to prevent him from wiggling out with a lie. If I alert anyone else…"

"It's liable to get back to him," Paula finished. Sighing then as well, she shook her head. "I'm out of my element here, Professor. My friend Sophie is the detective, not me."

"Which is why I wanted to see you about this."

"You want the police involved?"

Bormann shoved away the idea. "We aren't there yet—this could all be a misunderstanding, which is the second reason I'm playing this close to the vest. My nephew, Hayden, took over the management of my finances from his father, Hank's younger brother. When Hayden assumed control, safeguards were also put in place regarding my access and freedom with my finances. That freedom is how I was able to get in and look around in the first place. The safeguards are there should I ever become mentally incompetent to make certain decisions. I can't alert the family that I'm questioning activity until I have proof to back me up. Otherwise, I risk questions regarding my state of mind and I—"

"Risk losing access to your own damn money." Paula balled a fist, hating to see her mentor in such a bind. "You say you don't want the police in on this but that you called me because of Sophie?"

Bormann straightened. "Actually, it's her husband I'm interested in. He and his partners. I think his company, Joss Construction, is one of my nephew's clients that Hayden may be using my assets to do business with."

Again, Paula felt in danger of losing her lower jaw function.

"I believe my suspicions are spot on," Bormann continued. "I may even have evidence that could link Hayden to one of the properties and prove to his clients that he's dealing under the table."

"So you don't think his clients are acting under the table with him?" Paula asked.

"I'm willing to keep an open mind on that score. Still, I can't be sure that none of them are speaking out because they're unaware of the scam or because they're benefitting financially." Bormann's expression turned apologetic. "I hate coming to you with this, hon. I know Joss has a very respected name in the business. This isn't about bringing them down."

"I get it, Professor B. You need someone in your corner who can't be disputed." Paula stood then, considering the situation as she paced the broad area flooded with natural lighting from the bay windows lining that end of the room.

"Professor B, why do you think Joss might be one of your nephew's clients? Do you have any signed documents or—"

Miranda Bormann was already shaking her head. "Hayden was always a smart kid. I'd hoped he'd go into the law profession when he was younger, but I soon realized that he was lacking in character and would do nothing for the field except add to the heap of lawyer jokes we all know and loathe. He's too smart to go and leave signed documents lying around, but Joss is the only client I can suspect him of having. He hasn't even been seen meeting with anyone who could fit the bill." She blew out a laugh. "He hasn't even been seen meeting with Joss."

"Then how do you know about them?"

"Paula, I may live in Boston, but I've still got a lot of friends and former colleagues in Philly. Some of those friends have known Hayden since he was a baby. He was seen going into Joss. Of course he could've been there to use their restroom, but something tells me his visit was about more than that."

She nodded toward the folder Paula still held. "If you take a closer look, you'll see that Joss has never handled a job for my husband or his family. But as I said, Joss is a pretty impressive outfit. There was talk of moving some projects there a few years ago. I recall Hank saying something, but so far the family business hasn't broken ranks with Kincaid, which has been their contractor for decades. The company's founder, Weaver Kincaid, is married to my husband's cousin Doreen."

"So your nephew wouldn't have a reason to be there otherwise?"

Bormann nodded. "Not on family business, and I can think of only one other purpose. If I'm right, chances are strong that he was there to see Linus Brooks, and it's widely known that no deals are greenlit for Joss without Linus's approval. If you want in with Joss, you've got to go through Linus Brooks first. From what I hear, he's a hard man to go through."

Don't I know it. Paula kept her agreement silent.

"I'm sorry, hon." It was obvious that Bormann saw the despair shadowing Paula's honey-toned face. She pushed to her feet. "I believe we could use that coffee now. You're gonna have to bring more of that soon if it tastes as good as it smells!"

While Bormann returned to her kitchen, Paula's attention remained fixed on the folder. She sat there trying to figure out which was worse—talking to Linus about their past or about this present upset? Everything in her said he'd done all completely on the up-and-up.

Almost everything in her said that. There was a time she'd have leaped to his defense at the slightest hint of someone questioning his integrity. But now…it was as she'd told him on that beach in Mexico—the girl who would've killed for him if he'd asked her to was gone.

"It's got such a fabulous color and the fragrance is so rich!" Bormann called as she poured out the coffee.

Paula was searching her phone contacts. Linus wasn't among them, but Joss Construction had been programmed in when she and Santigo Rodriguez were finalizing the many surprises he had in store for his wife during their honeymoon.

The line was answered. "Joss Construction. How may I direct your call?"

Paula debated half a second longer and then sighed. "Linus Brooks, please."

Chapter 3

"So you're in?" Linus faked impatience while waiting on the man seated across from him to make a final decision on what he had just proposed.

Barker Grant sat with his chair pushed back from the table while he hunched forward. Elbows resting on his knees, his manner confirmed that he was in deep debate with himself.

"How long?" he asked.

Linus grimaced, taking pleasure in the man's torment. "Two, two and a half weeks tops."

Barker leaned back in the chair, giving a long, low whistle that had his dark rugged features relaxing with anticipation. "I could sure use some time like that."

"It's the age of technology, you know?" Linus said.

"We're all taking work with us, so there's no reason you can't too."

The intensity that so often held Barker's attractive face returned. "Work's the last thing I'd want to take along with me to The Bahamas."

"Seriously?" Linus whistled. "Never thought I'd ever..."

There was no need to finish the statement. Barker Grant was a die-hard workaholic if there ever was one. The award-winning hard-news journalist had a face made for the cameras, but his trademark scowl threw a wrench in those plans. The scowl's effect often ran more toward intimidation than invitation. Barker didn't mind; he was most fulfilled when he was digging up what others would prefer remain hidden.

"I'm not getting anywhere with the story I'm trying to put together," he said.

"Can I get a preview?" Linus asked.

Barker rolled his eyes and smiled. "Nothin' to preview. *Preview* means I'd need to have copy written. And folks would have to talk to me before I can write anything."

"Got it. So as far as the trip goes, all that's needed now is for you to say yes."

"So why is it a guys-only trip?" Barker seemed skeptical.

"We're working."

Something in Linus's answer seemed to trigger Barker's reporter's instincts, for he watched his old friend at length for several seconds.

"You can go on and say it," Linus urged in a dry manner.

"Nothin'." Barker gave a half shrug. "I'm just surprised Eli, Tig and Rook would want to go so far without taking their girls."

"Yeah, well." Linus waved to the waiter, indicating refills for himself and Barker. The two had gotten together for lunch at a pub just down the street from the courthouse. "That's the way they wanted it," he finished.

"They wanted it that way, huh?" Amusement joined Barker's knowing expression.

Linus didn't bother with a response. He merely waited on his old friend to get to the point he intended to make.

"You're no hermit, Line. I'd think you'd have more than a few lucky ladies you'd want to bring along on a trip like this."

"A business trip?"

"A Bahamas trip."

"There's no one, B."

"I get it." Barker's expression cleared of its suspicion as realization wedged in. "*You're* not bringing anyone. My love life's nonexistent. They're making it a guys' trip so we won't feel like complete losers, huh?"

"That's not it." Linus swore even as he burst into laughter. "We're welcome to bring someone. She doesn't have to be *the* one."

"So why aren't you—" Barker clipped his question when Linus suddenly bolted to his feet as if at attention. He didn't have long to wait to discover what had elicited such an alert response.

"Paula." Linus's liquid brown eyes were unwavering as DA Paula Starker approached the table.

"Hey, Linus." Paula's smile was there, but it was weak. Her efforts increased when she looked at who accompanied him. "Hey, Barker."

"Well, well, well!" Barker grinned broadly.

The gesture had Paula laughing within seconds. "No comment," she added and summoned a playfully wicked grin. It was customary for her to greet the reporter in such a manner. Customary but harmless. Paula had nothing but the highest regard for the way Barker did his job. The two of them shared a hug before she turned back to Linus.

"Sorry for interrupting you guys."

"No problem at all, Madam DA," Barker insisted as he reclaimed his seat. "Join us."

"Oh no thanks, Barker. I, um, can't stay. But please, please," she urged when Barker changed his mind about sitting.

Barker sat, but noticed his friend still stood at attention. The move spoke volumes.

"I tried to reach you yesterday," Paula was saying to Linus.

"Really?" Linus's stance lost some of its rigidness. "No one told me."

"It's fine. I—" she gave a quick shake of her head "—I didn't leave a message or my name when I called. They told me you were in a meeting so… We, um, I need to talk to you."

"Right." Linus gave a curt nod and looked to Barker. "B, I'll catch you later—"

"No, no, it's fine," Paula said. "I'm here for another meeting actually. I saw you when I got here and just thought I'd ask." She cleared her throat to quell the stab of need his fixed gaze had the power to induce.

"If you have time tomorrow—"

"Anytime," Linus interrupted her to accept. "I, um, I'm usually in the office by seven," he added.

"Seven." Paula seemed a little taken aback by the time. "Could we make it eight?"

"Yeah." Linus sighed as though he'd been holding his breath. "Yeah, that's fine."

"Thanks." She smiled and then squeezed Barker's shoulder before taking her leave.

The waiter was returning with drink refills when Linus finally reclaimed his seat. Barker enjoyed a few swigs of his beer before dissolving into a round of laughter.

"Jeez, Line, she was only in Mexico for a night."

It took a moment before Linus tuned into Barker's words. "What are you talking about?"

"Well hell, you've either slept with her or you want to—can't say I blame you for that." Barker glanced in the direction Paula had gone. "She's gonna leave the next DA with some damn big shoes to fill, but as for looks, I doubt her successor could even hope to compete in that department."

"It's not like that, B."

"Oh? So you *don't* want to sleep with her? Good to know...maybe I *will* bring someone along to The Bahamas." The idea carried no weight for Barker, but he felt it was worth it to see the slice of temper flash in Linus's eyes.

"Apologies, man," Barker quickly stated, knowing better than to upset his friend. "So what's up? Why so tense around her when she's obviously got a thing for you?"

His last words had the temper easing out of Linus's eyes to make way for curiosity.

"Really?" Barker grinned in disbelief. "You of all people—the ladies' man—and you didn't catch that?"

Linus shook off whatever flutters of hope were beginning to take root in his stomach. "You're off base here, B. We've got a history and it's not a good one."

"But she's the one, isn't she? The one you'd like to bring on this trip."

"I've got plenty of someones to choose from, remember?"

"True. But somehow I'm guessing that loses its shine when your best friends are bringing their special ladies."

"I'll never get her back, B. Eli and Tig think talking will do the trick. I think that too, but what happened between us...she's still hurting over it."

"Have you guys talked about it at all?"

"Not since it happened."

"Well hell, Line, don't be so quick to say you won't get her back then."

"You don't know what I did and said."

"I know she came to see you just now—she wants to talk. Who's to say things aren't about to change?"

Barker let his pep talk rest, seeing that the words were having a positive effect on the other man. Given that, he decided to move on to a different topic. "So…no women on this trip, huh? Exactly what else besides the weather are we supposed to look forward to?"

"Linus only stepped away for a moment, DA Starker, but he asked that I show you right in when you arrived."

"Thanks so much," Paula said to the woman who'd greeted her with enviable brightness just minutes before the 8:00 a.m. hour. "And please, call me Paula."

Estella Mays appeared both honored and horrified by the offer. "Oh, I couldn't—"

"Anyone who can convince every man in her family to vote a woman into the DA's office has surely earned the right to call me by my first name," Paula insisted.

Estella beamed. "The men in my family recognize intelligence and integrity when they see it. You weren't a hard sell."

"Thanks, Estella."

"Anytime…Paula. Now—" Estella headed into the office and waved for Paula to join her. She'd stopped next to a square serving cart that waited in the office living area. "Given the hour, Linus thought you might want a little breakfast."

Paula removed her coat. "That was sweet of him."

"I can't say how filling a breakfast it'll be," Estella cautioned. "These things don't look big enough to fill a gnat's stomach."

Paula was smiling as she joined the woman near the cart. She'd already recognized the invigorating aroma of her morning tea and didn't plan on turning down a cup. Her steps faltered a bit though when she saw what else had been provided in addition to the tea.

"He said they were your favorites." Estella's round, dark face still held signs of uncertainty.

Paula gave a jerky nod followed by a smile that hinted of remembrance as she reached out to brush her fingers along the damask cloth covering the cart. A round glass platter carried a generous supply of what had once been her favorite pastries.

"I hope it's not inappropriate to say I'm envious of your appetite."

"Oh, don't be fooled." Paula laughed over Estella's comment. "These little pastries don't allow for stopping at just one, but they're murder on the hips. Please." She waved toward the platter. "Come on," she encouraged when Estella looked ready to refuse. "It's the least I can do for such a valuable constituent." She smiled when the woman treated herself to one of the creations.

Sure enough, Estella appeared in ecstasy the moment the tiny pastry disappeared in her mouth.

Paula laughed, tickled by the woman's delight. "More," she offered, smiling. "If *I* have to finish this entire platter myself, I will, no questions asked."

"If you insist." Estella took a few more pastries and then firmly stepped back from the cart. "I couldn't take another. Linus made such a big deal about making sure we had a fresh batch on hand when you got here."

"He did?" Paula's hand hovered near the handle of the teapot. She listened while Estella relayed stories of how her boss had her calling all over town the day before, trying to find someone who could make the pastries.

"Seems the bakery that used to make them went out of business years ago."

"Yeah," Paula recalled, shaking off the memory of how weepy she'd gotten over the fact.

"Well, thank you for the samples." Estella clutched the napkin full of the treats close to her chest. "I think I've found a new friend to torture my waistline with. Call me if you need anything. Linus should be here soon."

Estella left, and Paula went about preparing a steaming cup of the tea. All the while, she forbade herself to even look at the pastries. Her willpower held less than fifteen minutes. She took a scant sip of her tea before setting aside the cup to zero in on one of the pastries.

"Damn you, Linus," she muttered when one of the tarts settled on her tongue.

The treats were about more than making sure she had something she'd enjoy for breakfast. He had to know she'd only be thinking of the nights she'd been up late either drafting or editing a motion for her boss, and Linus would arrive with a box containing several dozen of the decadent fruit-topped vices.

The bakery was a twenty-four-hour establishment in those days. The nights had passed with work forgotten and them in bed, with Linus feeding her from the box. Paula didn't need to ask herself what he was doing or what he was up to now. She knew very well. He'd been very straightforward about that in Mexico, hadn't he? He wanted to explain, but more than that, he wanted her back.

She washed down the last of the tart with a dose of the delicious tea. Once more, she forbade herself another taste of the pastry. They'd been her favorites since forever, something she had only allowed herself following an all-nighter that earned her an A on a paper. Her favorite delights hadn't come cheap back then, especially not for her pockets with the debt of law school on her plate. It had often been a struggle to keep a good supply of pantyhose. Satisfying cravings for something fresh, baked and decadent hadn't been a good idea for her budget.

Budget. The word made her smile. Money was required for a budget and she hadn't seen much of that until she landed her first associate's job.

That was after she met Linus though. She'd only been an intern then, with no business talking to clients, so she had kept her distance when he had visited her firm in those days. But keeping her distance hadn't meant she couldn't admire him from afar. And admire she had. The dark, sexy entrepreneur with the arresting eyes and dimpled chin had caught the attention of every female intern there, and an impressive number of the male ones as well.

He'd had to know he was to die for. Paula recalled thinking no man could be that beautiful and not realize the effect it wielded over others. Still, it had been important to look beyond the outer flash to what was less apparent. Miranda Bormann had taught her that. Paula had found herself using the technique to get a read on Linus Brooks back then. Rumor had been he was there on business for his construction outfit. Little had anyone known that business involved wooing several of the firm's associates to come work for the Joss legal department.

Linus's offer had been an impressive one, and he had wound up spiriting away new lawyers from firms all over the city. Though she had observed him from a distance, Paula remembered sensing something—a ruthlessness that was both subtle and intense. She'd supposed one needed such talents to be a success at most endeavors. She hadn't held it against him, especially given she had also sensed there was integrity at work. It had said a lot that he'd come right into the firm to speak with the associates he was interested in.

Later, Paula had learned he'd even spoken to the firm's partners. He'd only sought associates from firms with healthy intern pools. The hope had been that the partners would put some of those eager beavers in the newly vacated positions.

Paula had been one of the lucky recipients of those opened positions. She'd also been the one to interrupt Linus's meeting with the partners. Her immediate supervisor had asked to be notified when a dossier was ready for his signature. Her interruption had been viewed as a sign that Linus's plan had merit. One of the other partners had pointed her out as one of their brightest stars.

When Linus had left the meeting, he'd made a pit stop by Paula's cubicle to ask her out to dinner. She hadn't hesitated to accept. From there…well, her life had consisted of decadent pastries and…other delights far removed from bakeries. It had been obvious that Linus Brooks came from money, but he didn't wear it with an elitist air. Moreover, he was generous, thoughtful and compassionate about the welfare of others. It hadn't taken Paula long to fall hopelessly in love.

"Damn you, Linus," she murmured again, tossing willpower aside and indulging in another of the pastries.

Memories—some of them, at least—were beautiful, but they had their place. It was now the present, and she had to consider the fact that he could be into something shady with the likes of Hayden Bormann. She couldn't disregard Miranda Bormann's law school teachings then. She was to look beyond into what was less apparent. Compassion and generosity aside, she believed that what she'd sensed of his suave ruthlessness was still spot-on. Did it take precedence over the integrity she'd also sensed?

Paula shook off the thoughts in favor of gorging herself on more of the pastries. She was happy to discover they still worked wonders on calming busy minds. The miniature pastry cups were flaky, buttery and filled with either strawberries, apple slices or raspberries. How the baker managed to cut them so small yet detailed lent to their novelty and priciness.

She was softly moaning by the time the tenth pastry, one apple-filled, settled on her tongue. It was then she sensed she wasn't alone. Linus stood watching her from his office doorway. Arms folded over what she knew to be a superb chest, he rested along the doorjamb. He wore the same smile he had when they stood across from one another weeks earlier.

Paula brought a hand to her mouth and swallowed the rest of the pastry. She forbade herself to cough when a few morsels got stuck in her throat. Reaching for her cup, she gulped down the rest of the tea to wash it all down.

"Morning," she greeted him in a no-nonsense manner, knowing all the while how easily he could see through her facade.

Linus was the only one who had firsthand knowledge of how powerfully the treats affected her. The reaction was close to orgasmic. He had remembered that very well and had evidently made himself scarce in hopes of giving her a false sense of privacy. He had arrived in the office to find her in the grips of the delight he knew she'd find in the unexpected gift.

"Morning," he returned her greeting while pushing off the jamb and shutting the door at his back. "Good as you remember?" he asked.

"You know they are," she said.

"Guess you don't get that the way you used to."

She cursed him once again, that time in silence. Oh yes, he knew damn well what he was doing. He knew damn well where his provocative queries had her mind traveling.

"They aren't the only ones in the world." She found a small measure of delight when she noticed the wattage of his smile dimming just a fraction.

The effect didn't last long. "No," he said. The cunning allure of his smile returned, and with it, Linus's gaze flared with want and determination.

"But they're the best," he finished while rounding the square cart where she stood.

Paula told herself to hold her ground. *You're the woman, not the girl. You're the woman, not the girl,* she chanted. Already her legs were feeling syrupy and molten, as molten as the chocolatey color of his eyes. Other parts of her body reacted similarly and she told herself to get a grip. *He hasn't even touched you...yet.* He hadn't touched her, but that wasn't the overarching issue just then.

They hadn't been alone together like this in…hell, she couldn't remember. No, that wasn't true. She remembered all too well, and that was the problem. Linus was right; it wasn't easy to find pleasure in anything less than the best.

You're the woman, not the girl. She reiterated the chant.

Linus was acknowledging that very thing though in a much different way. Paula was the woman—all confidence, accomplishment and seductive presence. She enhanced the girl he'd lost his heart to. The one who unknowingly still held it a willing captive.

"With the bakery closed, I didn't know anyone was still making those." She shared the words in a rush while reaching for one of the Wet-Naps on the cart and cleaning microscopic crumbs from her fingers. All the while, she wished he'd say something. The way he stood there—dark, smoldering, with bone-deep sex appeal—had her seconds away from swooning.

"I had Estelle call around to some of the bakeries," he said. "I heard a few of them had come into the original baker's recipes when he retired."

Paula was stunned and forgot her unease over his closeness. "How'd you come by that news?"

"I was there when he had his going-out-of-business sale. The baker had no heirs, and the media made a big deal of highlighting the city's new talents who'd be featuring some of his most popular dishes in their menus." He shrugged. "I couldn't remember who got the one for his pastries."

Paula knew her amazement was thoroughly evident. "You actually went to something like that?"

Linus chuckled, the amber glints flickering in his gaze as amusement took hold. "I brought a heap of stuff back to the office for everybody to pig out on. Tig and Eli made gluttons out of themselves, but everybody walked away satisfied."

He seemed to sober then. "I only went because I thought you'd be there."

His admission tossed Paula back into reality. She finished with the Wet-Nap, tossing it into a nearby wastebasket en route to making a mad dash from behind the cart.

Her intentions were thwarted when he took her arm effortlessly. She was then tossed back to three weeks prior—Linus had taken her hand and she had thought she'd melt. Her reaction to him now was just as immediate and even more intense.

"Linus." Her voice carried on a breathy chord. "Don't do this."

"What?" Linus used phony confusion to his advantage. "This?" He massaged her upper arm as he moved closer.

Paula could only bow her head and just manage to mouth his name then.

"This?" he prompted, nuzzling the spot behind her ear while his free hand cupped her cheek.

"Or is it this?" He kissed her then, his tongue taking full possession in deliberate exploration.

The sudden rush of pleasure infused her bones in a surge powerful enough to bring her to her knees. But Linus had a firm grip to prevent that, and Paula chanted her silent reminders that she was the woman, not the girl.

Except the chants didn't help at all.

The girl was calling the shots, and the woman was happy to follow helplessly along. For a while, she made no effort to reciprocate the kiss. She was happy just relishing the sensation of having his tongue in her mouth. He made love to it as he would when he used his tongue to claim other parts of her body. He had a gifted tongue, and her persistent moans and shudders attested to that fact. It wasn't long before she was eagerly returning his efforts. Slowly, she joined him in their sensual dance, rotating his tongue with hers, treating it to a lazy suckle and smiling when he moaned in turn.

Linus shifted his hold then, taking Paula fully in his arms. Her shudders went into overdrive when she confirmed that his chest was still as superb as she'd remembered. Greedily, she splayed her hands across his muscle-packed torso while his roamed her back and hips. Quiet moans and gasps circulated in the air as their kiss intensified. Linus's hand loosely cupped her neck, while his thumb beneath her chin kept her mouth perfectly positioned for his.

His hand at her hip drifted, fingers taking hold of her pleated skirt until they were skimming the curve of her upper thigh and derriere. Paula's arousal hit a new high, along with her panic. She used her hands at his chest to push him away while she drank in huge streams of air until her heart rate slowed.

"Linus," she gulped while nervously pushing bobbed curls from her face. "Linus, I—I didn't come here for this." She swallowed determinedly, hoping to dislodge the lump that had made a home in her throat.

"I didn't come here for this, Linus."

"Right." He nodded as if to remind himself of what he already knew. "Right, we have to talk first. Paula, you have to know what happened that night had—"

"Linus, no, no, that's—that's not what I meant." Paula blinked as though she'd surprised herself by the outburst.

Following another steadying breath, she backed—or rather, stumbled—away to head for the chair in front of Linus's desk. She'd put her things there when she'd arrived. Linus moved from behind the cart, which had her putting a chair between them as she searched her tote for the reason she'd requested their meeting. Locating the black portfolio, she pulled it free and presented it. But Linus didn't accept.

"What is it?" he asked.

“What I came to see you about. What we—what we should be talking about.”

“And that is?”

“It’d be easier if you just read it.”

Linus’s features sharpened, and Paula felt the effects of the look dagger her heart. She understood very well then how he’d earned such a rep for no bullshit, for being a hard man to go through.

“You came to see me about business.”

It wasn’t a question. Paula nodded anyway, though still offering the portfolio.

“Business you can’t even discuss with me first,” he added.

“It’s better if you read this—just an overview, and then we can…talk.”

Linus approached and studied Paula again at length before taking the folder. He turned away to begin to read, and Paula turned away for a very different reason.

To finish recovering from his kiss.

Chapter 4

"You think I'm capable of this?"

Ten minutes later, Linus had read through the summary and, from what Paula could tell, had given it a second read. The portfolio contained an overview of her conversation with Miranda Bormann. The entry was a timeline of sorts, chronicling dates beginning with Bormann's initial discovery of the discrepancies regarding her finances, all the way to her nephew's suspected visits to Joss Construction.

"We just wanted to be thorough." Paula had even included a snapshot of Hayden Bormann.

Linus seemed to register no recognition of any of it. "But *you*? You really think I'd be party to something like this?"

"This isn't personal, Linus—"

"The hell it's not." He slammed down the portfolio and turned away in disgust. The intensity of his voice didn't match its volume, which remained quiet in its fierceness. He bowed his head, and Paula could see the muscle along his jaw working vibrantly.

"This isn't the way I do business."

"I know that, Linus—"

"Do you? Do you really?"

"Linus, please. I know you have a respected reputation."

A flicker of his earlier ease returned. "How do you know that?"

Her smile was cool as she shifted a shoulder. "A good DA knows what businesses contribute most heavily to her city's economy, and she knows who runs them."

"And still you come to me with this." He sent another disgusted look toward the folder.

"We were just covering our bases, Linus."

"And does it matter that I've never heard of Hayden Bormann? Or his aunt?"

"Like I said, we're just trying to cover our bases."

"Covering bases isn't easy." Linus considered. "Isn't this kind of work a little below your pay grade? This is the kind of work for an ADA and his team of assistants, isn't it?"

"I work just as hard as everyone in my office, and this is personal. I owe Miranda Bormann."

"Why?"

"She was my professor in law school. She's a good woman who doesn't deserve to be going through this—definitely not from someone in her very own family."

More of Linus's anger seemed to drift away. Paula could almost see the transformation taking place as understanding filtered into his expression. When he looked to the portfolio a third time, his expression held more curiosity than disgust.

"She's not out for blood, L. She just wants answers." Paula slapped her hands to her sides in a bewildered fashion. "She's holding out hope that there could be explanations here that go beyond shady dealings. If her nephew is up to something underhanded, she hopes his clients aren't involved, that maybe they're just unaware of what's really going on."

Linus had retrieved the folder. Again, he was scanning its pages.

"I know I could've been a little more up-front on what I wanted to talk to you about when I saw you yesterday with Barker—"

"You don't have to explain, Paula. Least of all to me." He raised the portfolio. "May I keep this?"

She waved toward it. "It's yours."

"What's your time frame on this?"

"We, um, we wanted to be thorough," Paula reiterated. "Professor Bormann says the questionable transactions only took place when she was out of town. She's not planning on taking any trips for a while. This is a personal matter so...we're on our own time."

Linus smiled. "You and Sophie must have the streets clear of crime if the DA has the kind of time to devote to something like this."

"I've got a good staff."

"Right. Another perk you'll miss?"

Paula gave a playful wince at his reference to their conversation in Mexico.

"So did I read that wrong, or have you really had your fill of the big chair?"

"It's not an easy job." She gave a refreshing smile. "It's like Professor B says—there are all kinds of ways to serve."

"She sounds like a smart woman."

"The smartest," Paula confirmed.

Linus gave another look to the portfolio. "I'll talk to my staff. Maybe they'll remember something I overlooked."

"Thank you, Linus." Paula began to collect her things. "And thanks for the pastries."

"Don't you want to know where I got them?"

"Hmph, my heart does. My hips might complain."

Linus's liquid brown gaze began an immediate assessment, and Paula refused so much as a flutter of her lashes while she endured it.

"Your hips have absolutely nothing to complain about," he said, smiling when Paula made a hasty departure.

"Well, well, don't you have work to be catching up on after all that time on your back?" Paula called out when she breezed into her office to find Chief of Detectives Sophia Hail-Rodriguez waiting to see her.

Sophia's gray eyes were alive with happiness and humor. "Oh! I wasn't just on my back. I—"

"Spare me." Paula raised a hand.

Sophia laughed as a sobering light crept into her

gaze. "I've been trying to decide whether to give you the cold shoulder after the way you just left me during the most perfect moment of my life."

"Well, your yummy husband hung around, didn't he?" Paula noted. "Doesn't get more perfect than that."

"Correct." Sophie inclined her head teasingly. "And he keeps trying to top himself on how perfect he can make things."

"That's what they're supposed to do, I hear." Paula rounded her desk and went to shuffle through the mail she found there.

"Too bad someone's making that difficult for him."

"Oh? How so?" Paula's question held an absent tinge as she continued to shuffle her mail.

"Tig's got an opportunity to get us away for a few more weeks of fun and sun, but it doesn't look like I'll get to go."

That caught Paula's attention. She took her chair then, eyes lawyer-sharp and expectant. "Something's up?" she asked.

"Oh yeah." Sophie sighed. "Trouble is, it's been happening right under my nose and I didn't know a thing about it."

"So we didn't get them all?" Paula shook her head, understanding Sophie referred to the members of law enforcement they'd already rounded up in connection to the money laundering racket they'd foiled.

"Nah." Sophia waved off Paula's guess. "*This* situation happened a long time ago. I guess me and my bestie aren't as tight as I thought. Otherwise, she'd have told me she was pining for a guy I've known almost as long as I've known my husband."

Realization had Paula rolling her eyes. Puffing out her cheeks as well, she stood and went to help herself at the bar near the floor-to-ceiling windows overlooking the city of Philadelphia.

"Why didn't you tell me?" Sophia asked.

Paula shrugged. "I don't know."

"Don't lie."

"Alright," Paula snapped, balling a fist. "If it didn't work out, I didn't want to have to talk about it. Especially with you. As it turned out, it didn't work out, so—"

"Whoa, whoa. What do you mean, 'especially with you'?"

"Let it go, Soph."

"Uh-uh." Sophia left her chair and joined Paula at the bar. "What is this? What's going on with you? Eli and Tig say L is a mess."

"Well damn, have you all just gotten together and discussed this?"

"Yes."

Even as Paula bristled in response to her answer, Sophia took pity. "Honey, we're sorry. We just love and care about you both. It's killing Tig and Eli to be so happy while Linus is so miserable."

Paula stilled. "Miserable?"

"According to them, he's been a mess since he saw you in Cortina."

"Oh please, you guys are making too much out of this now. Linus was just…caught up in the moment."

"And what about you?" Sophia challenged. "'Cause it's clear you aren't your usual take-the-world-by-the-scrotum self."

Paula sneered. "Thanks."

"Don't mention it. What I'd like you to mention though is why you wouldn't tell me of all people about Linus? Why would you think it wouldn't work out for you guys?"

"I didn't think that." Paula pushed back from the bar. "I wanted to marry him, and when it didn't work out that way… Sophie, I didn't tell you because whenever I've been really happy in my life, it's never lasted. I'm not just talking about with men, either. Linus, he… I've never been that happy. I don't think I've been as happy since."

Concern had Sophie frowning. "Honey, what happened?"

"That's just it." Paula's voice held an amused, bewildered tone. "I have no idea what happened."

"Well, didn't you want to—"

"Not anymore, Soph."

"Paula…" Sophie looked more uneasy. "You realize that with me and Tigo married, there's a chance you and Linus will run into each other a lot?"

"I know."

"Can you handle that?"

"Please." Paula looked offended. "'Course I can."

"Prove it. The guys have to go to The Bahamas. Tigo, Eli and Rook want to make it a couples trip for obvious reasons, but they don't want Linus to feel left out."

"Seriously?" Paula's offended expression sharpened.

"It's pretty low of you guys to hinge the fate of your sex trip on me."

"And yet here I am, doing it anyway."

"Why do I have to be there?" Paula sounded close to whining, and she didn't care. "I'm pretty sure that Linus won't be in any danger of being left without a date."

"Well, well, is that your way of acknowledging how dreamy he is? I'm surprised."

"I didn't acknowledge that."

"So you disagree that he's dreamy?"

"I didn't say that."

"You aren't saying much of anything, you know. What's wrong? Can't think with visions of Linus Brooks on the brain?"

Paula waved toward her office door. "If you have no official business to bring to the DA's office, Chief..."

"Mmm...pulling rank." Sophia looked smug. "My, my, you *are* frustrated. I think I know a guy who can help you with that."

"Soph, I swear—"

"Uh-uh-uh, no hitting the Chief of Ds..."

"I think I outrank you."

"I've got a better right hook."

"We'll see." Paula returned to the bar with intentions of finishing the drink she'd started to prepare.

"Honey, Linus doesn't want to go down there with anyone but you."

Paula blinked, then turned to consider her friend. "He said that?"

"According to Tig and Eli, it was pretty obvious.

Whatever you talked about in Mexico must've really gotten to him."

"Hmph." Paula returned to fidget with her glass. "I'm sure that's not the case after what I said to him this morning."

"Dare I hope you'll give me the scoop? Or is this more gossip I'll have to get from my husband?"

"Do you remember Professor Miranda Bormann?"

"One of your law professors? Sure."

"She's got some personal problems involving a shady nephew. He may be doing business with Joss." Paula took a seat on one of the bar stools. "Since Linus is the guy all new clients have to meet first—"

"You think Linus is into something dirty?"

"I didn't say that, Soph."

"So lemme guess, after your talk this morning, he believes that's exactly what you think."

"I just don't think I'm his favorite person right now, so… I should probably skip this little getaway. So should you." Paula pointed a finger in Sophie's direction. "Considering you've been away so much already.

"I calculate I'm owed more time." Sophie pointed out. "Besides, let's not forget we'll be deep in winter soon—better to get out while the gettin's good. But this is about more than sun and fun."

"Oh?" Paula pushed off the stool she occupied.

"Me and T think we've found the perfect way to repay Rook and Veev for Mexico. The place in The Bahamas is an island all to itself. There's an amazing villa less than ten miles from Finley Cay, near Nassau."

"Nice."

"I know, right? The guys have to take the trip anyway—a brainstorming session for ways to develop the island. The villa alone makes it a marvel—the perfect spot for one of my favorite couples to become man and wife. In the meantime, my other favorite couple can work on their issues."

"Soph—"

"I'll get more details to you soon. It's still another few weeks before we head out." Sophia went to her friend, took her by the shoulders and squeezed. "You've never quit a thing as long as I've known you. Don't wimp out now."

Paula knew it was pointless to argue, so she didn't.

Satisfied, Sophia nodded and then grabbed her coat and bag and prepared to leave. "If you're worried about you and Linus being the only unattached ones there, don't be. Clarissa's having this same conversation with Rayelle, and Linus already talked Barker into coming."

"This just keeps getting better and better." Paula sighed.

Sophia fixed her oldest friend with a stern look, and then she was gone.

"Paula?" Linus hesitated before completely abandoning the confines of the elevator. He felt it best to announce himself, or else risk a less cordial introduction to her security team.

"In the living room!"

Linus heard her call and used it to locate the space. His steps slowed. She'd called out with such familiarity that he wondered if she had gotten him confused with somebody else. He called himself a fool, remembering that he'd had to be announced before entering her place—or her elevator, to be more precise.

His past was against him, which was why he was neck-deep in guilt and self-consciousness. *She invited you up, idiot. Just be grateful and don't waste the chance,* he told himself. Linus made his way through the exquisite penthouse apartment. In spite of his uncertainty over being there, it didn't prevent him from appreciating the home. He'd always favored the craftsmanship of the building from the outside. He'd never had the chance, or rather, never taken the chance, for a closer inspection.

Once he'd been told that the residence was home to the DA—his estranged former love—he'd steered clear. Now, he had confirmation that the interior was equally impressive. The color scheme ran in warm browns and rich cream enhanced by glossy woods, some of which were trimmed in brass and bronze.

The place was a fine balance of male comfort and female elegance. Linus found Paula surrounded by gorgeous art and body-pampering furniture. She appeared anything but relaxed hunched over her laptop, which was perched on a square pine coffee table before a long overstuffed sofa and matching armchairs. She and her tote bag occupied one of the chairs.

Linus couldn't hide his smile and didn't try to. How could he, when she was every bit of a reminder of long-ago evenings when he'd drop by her more modest apartment to find her in the midst of meeting an encroaching deadline? Linus bowed his head then, clearing his throat as the memory turned down a different path. Deadline or not, he'd have had her naked and moaning less than an hour after his arrival.

She was watching him suspiciously as he left the memory behind.

"I see you still have something against using a desk," Linus said, deciding she wouldn't appreciate knowing where his thoughts really rested.

Paula took stock of her area. "I can promise you my desk at work gets lots of use. Did you find out anything?"

She'd leaned back in her chair to watch him, and Linus's mind was a total blank. A total blank if he didn't count his brain rapidly firing as he assessed the lush line of her legs and thighs that were bared by the oversized 76ers T-shirt she sported.

Paula straightened suddenly, reading Linus's assessment all too clearly then. He snapped to as well and moved deeper into the room.

"There's nothing to report," he said, "but my staff's on it, and they're very thorough." That was the only bright spot in the entire mess, Linus mused. He was counting on the thoroughness of his staff to give him more time with the woman he cursed himself daily for losing.

"If there's anything to find, they will." He moved farther into the room. "I've got them going over all current jobs and those completed in the last year."

"Thanks, Linus. Professor B will be glad to hear it."

Linus smiled. "You guys seem close."

"We are." Paula's smile was laced with memory. "She was very good to me. In ways I can never repay."

Linus decided to turn the conversation before the air grew too heavy with past regrets. "Paula, about this morning—"

"Forget it." Heat swept her, and she pushed away from the armchair. "A kiss is the least I could give you for those pastries."

"Glad to hear that." A shallow furrow took shape between Linus's long, heavy brows. "I'm actually talking about the way I acted when you got to the point of your visit. I haven't lost my temper, *really* lost it, since that night—"

"Linus—"

"I shouldn't have reacted the way I did this morning. You're trying to help someone you care about. I definitely get that, in spite of what you might think of me personally."

Paula didn't know what to say and prayed he'd say more.

"I came here to tell you that. We, um, we may have to see each other a few times before this is all over, and I don't want…any more drama between us."

Paula nodded, and a small burst of laughter escaped. "No, we sure don't need any more of that."

"I hear Sophie talked to you about the trip."

Further amused, Paula scooted deeper into her chair. "Talked to? Ordered me is more like it."

"Will you follow her orders?" Linus strolled over to the mantle to enjoy the pictures of Paula and Sophie that lined it.

"Doesn't look like I have a choice." Debate crossed her face then. "Sounds like you do though."

Curious, Linus turned to study her.

"You're free to take whoever you want, L, because now that Sophie knows we…have a past, she's on a mission to *fix* us. All this wedding planning and love-conquers-all stuff is going to her head."

"It's not the worst thing to have go to your head, you know?"

Paula huffed. "Well, just because I have to suffer doesn't mean you should."

"I won't be suffering, Paula. At least not because I'm not getting what I want out of this trip."

Paula shook herself free of the ability his eyes had to take hers captive and suspend her in desire. "You know, you really shouldn't bother driving all the way across town while we solve this Bormann thing." She latched onto the topic at the forefront of her mind. "We can cover most of this by phone."

"And your professor is sure her nephew came to see me?" Linus had already dismissed her suggestion to handle business any other way but in person.

"She's not sure of much. She has to be careful who she asks, or she'll get certain members of her family involved before she's ready to. According to the private investigator she hired, her nephew's been seen visiting Joss. Understandably, the guy couldn't go in asking questions about who Hayden Bormann was there to see."

"So naturally it's me."

"Linus, I'm—"

"It's alright. I didn't mean anything by it. Tig and Eli have no clues about this guy either." Sighing, Linus massaged all ten fingers into the nape of his neck. "That means whoever this is hasn't gotten past me to the client stage."

Paula noticed a more pensive look take hold of his fierce features. "What?"

"The trip we're putting together in The Bahamas is really about business." Linus shook his head over the irony. "We have a ton of proposals we've been debating for a while now."

"Debating?"

"That's another way of saying Eli and Tig have questions. Usually I'm the one with doubts—picking apart every detail to find a weak spot."

"Which is why you guys always turn out A-rated properties."

Linus appeared surprised by the compliment.

"I'm only repeating what the word is around town. They're lucky to have you," she said, thankful he released her from his steady gaze before she began to squirm beneath it.

Linus shrugged, his friends and partners taking his focus again. "For one of us to have hesitations is cause for a proposal to go on the TBD pile. Tig and E are big picture guys, which you need in a business like ours, but too many businesses like ours have fallen by the wayside because they overlooked details that came back to bite them in the ass." He shook off the idea.

"Anyway, this stack of proposals is what we hope to get through during the trip. I've got my staff looking at past and current jobs, but not these. I'd be happy to let you take a look at them if you want."

"Yeah." Paula looked surprised and pleased by the offer. "It'd be great, especially if I find something and I know it's nothing you guys have put your hands on yet."

"We have everything printed in hard copy, but I could get it to you on a drive if that works better," he offered. "We should probably avoid couriers and such. Best to keep this in as few hands as possible."

"Agreed." She shook her head in wonder then. "Linus, thanks."

"Not a problem." Something shifted, intensified in the way he studied her. "I'll drop it by your office around noon tomorrow." He made the offer, hoping to work in time alone with her during the lunch hour.

Paula's eyes brightened with acceptance and then dimmed almost a second later. "I've got a working lunch with my staff tomorrow at Dugall's."

Linus whistled, thinking of the posh establishment with only private dining rooms. "A lady who knows how to treat her staff."

Paula waved off the implication that she overindulged her people. "It's only on special occasions." *Like letting my people know their boss is calling it quits,* she tacked on silently. "We should be done by one, one-thirty. I could swing by after."

Disapproval rimmed Linus's gaze. "That's a hike, Paula. How 'bout I just drop it off for you there at Dugall's. That's easier for you, isn't it?"

"Yeah, um, yeah it would be," she accepted and prayed she didn't sound as eager as she felt. *Paula...*

She could practically hear the berating tone she often used to call herself down.

The man was dangerous, she reminded herself. He was dangerous in a subtle, seductive manner that approached determined, yet deliberate. That manner teased and tempted his quarry until she was naked and moaning beneath him. Linus Brooks making it "easier for her" had so many connotations. They made her head spin while every other part of her throbbed.

"Thanks again, Linus.

"You're welcome. Why'd you come see me about this?" He posed the question on the same breath.

Despite its suddenness, the question didn't surprise Paula. If he was as instinctive as she'd heard, and by now pretty much believed, she was certain that the question had occurred to him since before she'd left his office that morning.

"Well, you said everyone has to come through you first, right?"

"But you didn't know that, or did you?" He slipped both hands into his trouser pockets while regarding her coolly. "You seem to know a lot about the way I handle my business."

Paula barely attempted a shrug. "Nothing strange in that given what's going on here, what we're investigating."

"So that's why?"

"What difference does it make, Linus?" She closed her eyes, using everything inside her to tamp down a sudden urge to moan. Jeez, the girl was making yet another steadfast climb to the upper levels of her conscience.

Paula scooted to the edge of her chair, but her moves weren't fast enough. Linus was there, blocking her way when he took his place before her on the edge of the coffee table. It took him no time to set her work materials on the sofa.

"Why'd you come to me at all?" he probed. "It would've been easier for you to take it to Eli or Tig, right?"

"Would you please stop with the 'easier for me'?" She tried again to scoot from the chair.

"Why? It would've been, right?" His fingers curved around the backs of her knees, keeping them apart and immobile.

Paula labored to shove aside the sensation his touch ignited. "I didn't want to worry them with this if there was no need—"

"But worrying me was alright?"

"I didn't much care if you were worried or not."

He grinned, appreciating the dig. "Somehow I didn't think you of all people would want to see me upset."

"But that seems to happen regardless, doesn't it?"

"Did you miss me, Paula?" His question countered hers, and he smiled when the truth he wanted to see flickered in her bright eyes.

Paula bristled again, drawing on everything she had to fight against emotion. "What difference does it make?" Her voice was a gasp.

"Because I miss you."

She shook her head, knowing that she was working to convince herself instead of him. "It's too late."

"Is it?" Linus used one hand at her knee to keep her still and accessible to him. The other roamed her inner thigh until he was cupping her core. His thumb commenced a lurid assault on her clit beneath her panties.

"Linus." She was melting for him, but if she accepted what he offered—what she wanted—and lost him again, it would crush her.

"Why won't you let me talk about that night?"

"I'm not the girl you want."

Linus took a knee before her then. He used his wide frame to keep her open for him. "You're wrong. You've always been the girl for me." He spoke at her collarbone before his divine mouth cruised the line of her neck and he sucked her earlobe.

Paula cursed the whimper she heard coming from her throat. It didn't stop her from nuzzling her ear against his mouth, angling it to gain more of his attention. Still, she was desperate to keep some semblance of the upper hand.

"She—she's gone, Linus."

"Is she?" He rotated his thumb while increasing the pressure of his treatment at her ear.

"Is she?" He murmured the question this time. His mouth traveled from her lobe to her jaw and finally the corner of her mouth. There, he nibbled and sucked her bottom lip until she granted him access.

The deep, steady thrusts of his tongue had her offering quiet wavering moans and instant participation. Paula met his thrusts with her own, all the while shifting to claim greater attention from his skillful thumb at her crotch.

Linus wanted her closer too and stood to accomplish that. In the midst of their kiss, her honey-toned thighs curved about his lean waist to lock him in a lush embrace. He broke the kiss then, hungry for the fragrance that clung to her skin.

"It's just down the hall," she said.

"What is?"

"Where I sleep." Her tone was innocent in its simplicity.

Far from innocent, Linus's grin was a devilish one. *Not tonight*, he vowed.

Chapter 5

She had him stripped of his suit jacket and shirt by the time they'd made it to her bedroom. There was no need to hold on for support as he carried her down the long, electric-candle-lit corridor that only led toward one destination.

His strength had always been a turn-on, even when it was terrifying. Paula gave a mental shove to wedge the idea from her thoughts. She would not linger there. Not in that part of the past. Not tonight.

Lashes unsettled with girlish fluttering, she inclined her head to leave Linus's mouth more room to play. He didn't let the offer go to waste. His teeth nibbled and grazed; his tongue lingered on her collarbone and the silken dip at the base of her throat.

When they arrived in the suite at the end of the hall,

Linus barely took a second to scan the room. His route was set once he located the bed, a king-sized oasis occupying a round, sizable platform in a far corner. A voice in his head—a faint one that wasn't too hard to stifle—reminded him that there were other things, *issues*, they should be focused on. They'd get there; there was no other plan besides that one—the one that involved them getting back together—as far as he was concerned.

Still, Linus knew he'd have to have Paula's cooperation to see that endeavor through. Unfortunately, she was against any conversation that addressed their past. Linus didn't blame her; only, until they dealt with said past, there was no future for them. And he'd settle for nothing less than a future with Paula Starker. If the physical level was the only plane she'd meet him on, so be it. He'd happily give whatever she asked of him. In the midst of their bliss, he'd make her listen to him. Listen to him or forfeit the pleasure he'd have her craving again and willing to do anything to satisfy.

At least that was the way he *hoped* it'd turn out. Forfeiting himself pleasure wasn't a part of the plan he would look forward to enacting. Linus spanned the platform steps and rested back against the generously pillowed headboard once he eased them down to the bed. He straddled Paula across his lap and let his forehead drop to her shoulder when her sex was nudging his. He groaned, and the sound brought a curious smile to Paula's mouth.

"You sound tortured, Mr. Brooks."

Her playful acknowledgment had Linus resting his head back, eyes closed. When he opened them, Paula's lashes fluttered anew with the sensation evoked by the sultry potency of his gaze.

"What?" she queried, watching while he grinned.

"I didn't come here for…this. Didn't come…prepared."

She smiled, slightly tilting her head. "I see." With that, she leaned over to pull open a drawer on the bedside table that was fashioned of the same creamy wood as the platform and bedframe.

Linus peered into the open drawer to discover, among other things, a generous supply of condoms. "What a lucky guy I am," he said. "They're all my size." He took out a few of the packets.

Paula shrugged half-heartedly. "It's the only size I buy."

Aside from the rigid set of his jaw, Linus's expression was unreadable. "Don't you worry about offending a guy who doesn't measure up?"

"If they're offended, they don't need to be here." She enjoyed the way his jolting stare strayed across the assortment of toys littering the drawer. "Are you offended?" she asked.

Linus didn't supply an immediate answer. He wasn't offended, but he was pissed. Thankfully, however, he was able to stop before torturing himself with questions of how many men she'd taken to her bed. All that mattered then was where he had her now.

Paula pulled her shirt over her head, leaving her in nothing but lacy gold panties hugging her hips. "Are you too offended to stay?" She tweaked her earlier question.

"I'll deal with it." In seconds he was resuming their kiss.

Paula cupped his face, languishing in the feel of his flawless shave beneath her fingertips. He kept her occupied with the act, scraping the roof and sides of her mouth until he'd enticed her tongue to tangle with his. Her responses were breathy moans that filled the room alongside choked gasps that kept time with the deft strokes his thumbs applied to tend her breasts more appropriately.

Paula rested her hands above her head and arched her back so that he'd leave no part of her breast untouched. Linus hadn't intended to. He suckled her nipples until they glistened and puckered for more. His lips and tongue plied her areolae and the surrounding mounds with wet open-mouthed kisses.

Paula let her memory surge, allowing glimpses of similar moments to take residence closer to the surface. Back then, she'd believed no one could surpass Linus's skill in the bedroom. Later, she had told herself those were just the ideas of an inexperienced girl. Now, years later and leagues away from inexperienced, she realized her perspective was right-on. He was still a thorough lover.

"L." The letter was wrapped in a sob when she felt his mouth on her sex.

Panties long gone, his hands had taken their place at her hips. His lips feathered over her clit before the tip of his tongue explored the tightly packed bundle of nerves. Paula squirmed, and he gave her hips a warning squeeze but didn't abandon his task. Linus fixed on the hypersensitive nub and only treated her moist folds to brief brushes from his lips.

It was enough. When his tongue circled the bud and sucked, Paula knew she was moments away from coming apart. Linus must've known that too, for that's when he stopped. He put Paula on her stomach before she could lash out. Instead of a verbal gripe over his tactics, she was releasing a muffled moan into one of the many pillows that were strewn across the bed. On his knees, Linus smoothed a hand over and under her hip and took possession of her core. His free hand cupped a breast and kept her secure off the bed and against his chest to give his fingers more room to play.

Paula, so erotically restrained, had no choice but to take what he subjected her to, the way he subjected her to it. It was a choice she highly approved of. His thumb took on the task of working her clit while his middle finger claimed her core as it grew wetter.

Lightly, he gnawed her shoulder, ego humming as her appreciative gasps filled the room. Proof of her pleasure doused his skin, coating the finger thrusting in moisture. She was more than ready for him, yet the tiny hiccupping sounds she made as he took her were hard to put an end to. Besides, the persistent clutch and release of her intimate muscles around his finger pulled his attention to how tight she was.

The memory of what she'd felt like when he'd claimed her virginity kept him suspended between the past possession and the one he now ached to reinstate. He flipped her onto her back and resumed the fingering as well as the kissing. With his free hand, Linus undid his belt and trousers, kicking free of them along with his boxers, socks and loafers.

Blindly, he smoothed a hand across the tangled peach comforter in search of the condoms he'd already pulled out. With expert efficiency, he tore a packet in half and applied protection. Paula could feel her heart lodged squarely in her throat when he pulled her to the center of the bed. Her eyelids felt heavy, drugged, while his thumbs massaged her folds, spreading them to accept him.

Linus took her swiftly, unapologetically possessive, as if to remind her of how woefully lacking her sex life had been since his absence. Her eyes flared in surprise before they returned to their drugged state. The only indication she gave of discomfort was the small grimace that curved her mouth once Linus filled her with every rock-hard inch of his wide sex.

Paula could actually feel the organ spreading her walls as it speared deeply, deliciously. She wanted to lock her legs around him and take him impossibly deeper. Linus prevented her, keeping his hold secure at her spread thighs. Slowly, he pumped his hips, rotating them ever so slightly to send waves of sensation vibrating through them both.

The pleasure was shattering. Paula treated Linus's thighs to the same massaging touch he did hers, though she was nowhere near capable of covering the expanse of his. His limbs were onyx dark and cut with muscle, much like his sex—strong and coaxing as it took all she had to give.

Paula labored to drive down the rushes of her impending climax. She wasn't at all ready for the moment to end. Linus released one of her thighs to brace his weight on a fist in the covers. He caged her beneath his body, which was toned and sleek as a living weapon. Awed by the planks of chiseled abdominals and generous pectorals, she reached out to pair touch with the sensation that sight had roused.

The stimuli was abundant and incomparable, their mutual moans of elation heightened. Linus's perfectly defined body took hers with such deft mastery. Paula's skin glistened from a mix of exertion and his kisses. The urge to climax hit her hard, and she could feel the unmistakable ooze of need pooling beneath her bottom. His erection showed no signs of losing its…capacity. His strokes remained consistent and unquestionably satisfying.

"I'm not done yet, DA Starker," he murmured while his tongue outlined a ripe, honey-brown nipple.

Paula's laughter melded with a moan. Her body was instantly primed for more.

He woke before she did, with no plans to leave. He had to, of course. In spite of what they'd spent the better part of the night indulging in, they were still nowhere close to being anything other than old flames enjoying missed activities. Paula was still in deep sleep, and Linus celebrated the fact.

Leave it alone—walk away—chalk last night up to one final spark between old lovers…

Though the silent voice grated on his nerves, he knew it spoke the truth. There was still time to walk away—to let things rest between him and Paula as they had for the last several years.

And then what? Go back to his life and watch as she went back to hers? Perhaps. That might've worked before. After last night though…did he really think he could walk away from her after that? Did he really believe that his carefully constructed rage management wouldn't obliterate under the pressure? It would. He knew that better than he knew what he'd have for breakfast that morning. All it would take would be for him to see her handling the simplest task such as grocery shopping, or something more involved and outrageous, like being on the arm of her latest newsworthy squeeze, and he'd lose it. He'd lose it simply over the fact that she wasn't his.

Last night though, she had been his—all his, and he wanted to keep it that way. There was no place in his realm of tolerance for him to watch her with anyone else after last night. There was, of course, a price to having her back—to having her be all his. He had to give her the truth about that night. The entire truth? He was still debating on how much of himself he would have to—or was ready to—lay bare to her.

He skimmed the back of his hand down her bare back and shook his head in approval of its silken quality and of the woman herself. He knew she'd settle for nothing less than the complete story. It was who she was, and he couldn't blame her for that curiosity. Despite his unwillingness to make a return dive into his past, he knew that when all was said and done, he could settle for nothing less than giving it to her.

Hating the plan but knowing it was his only recourse, Linus reluctantly shoved away the covers. He allowed the back of his hand one last skim across her shoulder before he forced himself from the bed.

Chapter 6

When Paula forced her eyes open that morning, she was greeted only by the shambled mess that had become her bedroom. There was no sign of Linus. Good.

It was good, wasn't it? She was glad he was gone, wasn't she? It was best that he was gone; there was no doubting that. Having him there when she woke, indulging in the aftermath rituals of soft talk, cuddling and future planning...it'd be too much. They weren't there yet.

Correction. They weren't there—period. End of story. The voice in the back of her head called that a load of bull. The accusation was met by a muttered curse from Paula as she kicked her legs free of the covers that still managed to cling to the mattress.

It had to be the end of their story—she wouldn't survive another blow that took him away from her. Better to go on doing without him than to risk losing him again.

Who says that would happen?

Paula curled her fingers into her hair, hoping to stifle another query she didn't want to answer. The fact was, Linus couldn't be part of her life until she knew what it was that drove him out of it in the first place. He was prepared to tell her that story, but she couldn't, *wouldn't* let go of past fears and heartbreak long enough to let him. Sure, she feared losing him again—he was a man a woman would kill to have. She'd even told herself that the woman inside her was in control and that she'd gotten over him.

None of that was at the heart of it though. It wasn't even at the foundation of it. Hurt feelings were at the foundation of it. Talk about the little girl inside making a comeback! What the hell was that about?

Hurt feelings were the very last thing she should be allowing to wage war on her thoughts. She was the DA, for goodness's sake! And yet…there they were. She'd let Linus Brooks in all the way, and when she had been at her most trusting, her most vulnerable…

Paula shook her head. She wouldn't allow it. No way would she let him just work his way back into her head and her heart, follow it up by a sob story and apologies and have things be the way they were. To hell with that.

And last night?

Again, the smug voice made its presence known. Paula couldn't deny it an answer this time. Last night, the girl and the woman were of one accord. She'd wanted every millisecond of what Linus had given her and more. Admitting that, giving in to that, didn't mean he suddenly had carte blanche status with her heart again, did it? Hell no, it didn't.

She tried to tug her pillow free from a corner of the dresser, stood and kicked the pillow instead. No, it did not mean that, and still…she knew that somewhere tucked away deep, a part of her was overjoyed by what had happened between them last night. A part of her was overjoyed by the fact that there was much more at work the previous night than consenting sex based on need and mutual attraction. It was a part that operated on a level that surpassed womanly sensibilities and girlish desires.

It was the part that knew she'd been making love to the man she loved. Giving in to Linus last night didn't mean he suddenly had carte blanche status with her heart again. It meant his status had never been revoked. Whatever aspects of the past still needed tending to, in reality they held no ruling over her heart and what it wanted despite the wounds it had endured.

Paula supposed keeping his story at bay was her last attempt at maintaining some level of her dignity, her control. She couldn't control the fact that she was still a sap for him. Refusing to let Linus ease his conscience by explaining that night allowed her to uphold the illusion that she wasn't. Petty, but it was all she had. Even sadder was the fact that she wasn't at all convinced she'd uphold the illusion the next time she saw him.

Which would be later that day, she mused, recalling the plan they'd made last night. He was to provide her with more material regarding the Miranda Bormann case. Linus was dropping everything off to make it "easier for her."

Paula gave her pillow another kick and went to throw herself back on the bed. Meeting him was not a great move if the plan was to drive out images of them together. The sheets were still fragrant with them. She moaned as their activities replayed in her mind with brilliant clarity. Instead of stripping the bed of its dressing and memories, she turned her face and inhaled to her heart's content. She'd tell him it couldn't happen again—that was her only option. The only one that would keep her sane, anyway. She'd resist him. She could do it—she knew she could. She was no weakling. She was the DA, dammit!

The phone on the night table was ringing. With the reminder of who she was fresh on the brain, she answered with stern impatience coloring her voice.

"Starker," she all but snarled.

"Good morning to you too," Linus greeted. "Are you okay?"

Her heart seized. "I'm fine." She celebrated the strength of her response. There was no need to speak of the throbs and slight lances of pain that shot through her core when she moved...or heard his voice through the phone.

"I didn't mean to leave you to handle that mess we made of your bedroom," he said. "You were sleeping so deep, I didn't want to wake you."

"Not a problem," she said breezily. It was true, and she'd never been more grateful to have a housekeeping service than in that moment.

"Listen, Linus—"

"What happened last night doesn't change anything, Paula. You're gonna have to hear me out, and you will. See you later."

The dial tone buzzed and then transitioned to the annoying busy signal. Only then did Paula realize she was still holding the receiver.

Dugall's was heavily frequented by those in Philadelphia's political circles. During the day, its patrons were a mix of political and law enforcement figures from various levels of stature. Dugall's lunch hour was said to be the place where such figures lost the shackles of their jobs and gathered like regular people who held profound respect, admiration and affection for one another.

The dinner hour was rumored to be much the same, but it was usually those figures with the greatest influence that patronized the five-star restaurant during that time. No matter the hour, however, Dugall's was notoriously hard to reserve for a table. However, figures like the mayor, police commissioner and district attorney avoided such difficulties, as there were always private dining rooms at their disposal.

Paula got a kick out of treating her staff to meals at the establishment. The successful prosecution of a case was always cause for a meal there. Most of her staff didn't make enough to dine there with any sort of frequency. She enjoyed showing them the nicer aspects of the careers they'd chosen.

Their dedication to the job gave Paula confidence that many of them would be among the dealmakers and legislators who would keep the city safe, secure and thriving. As she observed the expressions at the wide round table, Paula saw uncertainty illuminating their usually eager faces. Her decision not to run for reelection had received virtually no positive response. She commended herself on making the announcement so far in advance. With luck, her group would have time to get used to the upcoming changes before they actually took effect.

Fortunately, the culinary talents of Dugall's chefs were most successful at lifting the spirits of her downcast staff. Paula had been able to get the unfortunate news out of the way before the second round of drinks arrived. The group was about halfway through a generous array of heavy appetizers when the first streams of laughter began to color the room.

The remainder of the meal carried forward on a chord of good vibrations that peaked once the normalcy of shoptalk got underway. Afterwards, the group walked—or, more accurately, waddled—from the dining room on full stomachs they didn't have to pay a dime to earn.

Paula stayed behind, having told her assistant she'd see her back at the office. She was in no mood to call Linus's bluff about seeing her there, so she used the time to get work done. At least, she tried. In the end, she resorted to making a few calls. She hoped that having someone else to talk with would add to the illusion that work was why she waited, and not because she was eagerly anticipating his arrival.

"The fact that there wasn't much press early on in the investigation is why it ran as smoothly as it did, Don. That might not be as easy this time around."

Paula paced the far corner of the dining room while speaking with Lieutenant Donald Weiss. The dining table had been cleared of dishes and now resembled a workspace, with an assortment of pens and legal pads littering it. It would've appeared that Paula and her colleague had butted heads more than once, but they'd become a surprisingly effective duo while clearing Philadelphia's streets.

A sigh passed through Weiss's end of the line. "There's already speculation in certain circles on this, Paula. To remain silent might give those circles the impression there's something to hide here. We're too fresh off that money laundering thing to risk that," he said.

Paula grimaced, although she somewhat agreed. "Do we need to decide this now? There's a chance this could involve a portion of our demographic best left out of the news. I don't give a damn about the impressions of certain circles."

Don chuckled. "Do you ever?"

"Jokes, Don? You don't want a personal visit from me, do you?"

"Is that a trick question?"

Paula's laughter caught in her throat when she saw Linus just inside the room, his back against the closed door. How the hell a man his size maneuvered so quietly, she was sure she'd never know.

He wore the same quietly amused smile he'd had on the beach just shy of a month ago. Paula kept her expression schooled, refusing to let him know it got to her as much now as it had then. Something told her she was wasting her time and that he already knew.

She tuned back in to Don, who was still going on

about the case. "I've got another meeting about to start, Don. You'll hear from me soon—promise."

"Your guys said to come on in," Linus explained once she'd disconnected.

Paula nodded. "I told them I was expecting you."

Linus tilted his head toward her mobile. "Hope I didn't interrupt."

"Difference of opinion with a cop."

"Didn't sound like he minded too much."

Paula decided it best not to follow up the comment, so she waited. Linus pushed off the door while pulling a small rectangular case from his trouser pocket. He placed it on the round dining table.

"Info as promised," he said.

Paula acknowledged it with a glance. "Pretty convenient. You guys just happening to have a group of jobs you felt uneasy over."

Linus's smile grew wider, as though he'd been waiting for the question to be raised.

"I hope this...info isn't just meant to keep me occupied when you're not in my bed." Her tone was deceptively polite.

Linus's tone mirrored it. "Is that an invitation?"

"I thought it sounded more like an accusation," she noted.

"Of what, exactly? That I'm trying to seduce you out of being suspicious of me?"

"I couldn't have asked that better myself."

"Will you answer?"

"What for? Sounds like you already have one you're comfortable with."

"Offended?"

"Satisfied. I was hoping we'd get this out of the way before the trip."

"Because it messes with the sleeping arrangements." His smirk carried no humor then. "Please tell me you don't believe this is just about sex for either of us."

"It was for me."

"Lies."

"Don't flatter yourself, Linus."

"I don't have to. You did that well enough last night. Or don't you remember?"

"I enjoyed myself, and I let you know it. This had nothing to do with—with anything else."

Linus broke into full-bodied laughter. "Baby, do you know who you're talking to?"

"Oh, I'm sorry, is this where you remind me that you were my first?"

"I don't think you need much reminding. My guess is that a great many of those hot and heavy dates that get so much press in the society section end right there in that splashy lobby where you keep your penthouse."

"Now you really are flattering yourself."

"Oh, don't get me wrong, Paula. I know I'm not the only one you've given a ride up in that elevator of yours. My guess is there haven't been many though." Linus forced himself to bite back his temper surging over the idea that there had even been one.

Paula regarded him with an unreadable twinkle in her eye and then smiled. "It's true. You know me quite well—the girl I was, and oh how she thought she knew you." Her smile sharpened when she saw his smugness dial back several notches.

Paula began to stroll the sizable dining room. "Yes, she thought she knew you too. She was so young and happy and overwhelmed by love that she romanticized her boyfriend by using words like *passionate*, *outspoken*, *driven* and *determined* when she described him." Paula feigned surprise then. "Oh, that's right. Us girls from the hood know those words too."

"Paul—"

"We have dreams. We want to be wives and doctors and lawyers and every other damn thing folks think we aren't worthy of because of where we come from."

"I know that, P."

"'Course you do. You know everything, don't you? You knew I was a gold digging bitch—that was the phrase, wasn't it? One of them, anyway."

"Please let me explain—" He moved toward her, but cut himself short when she retreated and added a minute shake of her head to further deny him.

"You think that night was the first time I saw that quick temper of yours, L? It wasn't. Back then, I called it passion. You know so much, Linus? Then surely you know girls often use that term to describe boyfriends who really are just plain jackasses."

She stormed to the table and shoved everything into her tote, including the drive he'd brought her. She headed for the door. "Enjoy the room. I'm done with it." She left him with a scathing look and then she was gone.

Paula thought she'd done a fine job of making it from the restaurant to the car and through her residence's lobby without giving away any hints as to the state of her mood. She recalled her "private" elevator had cameras and made sure to wear a closed expression on the way up.

Once she'd exited into her foyer and the doors had bumped shut at her back, she dropped the facade. An anguished sound left her throat as she stripped off her coat and hurled it across the floor. Viciously, she tugged a hand through her hair and cursed. She hadn't meant for it to go so far.

But it was what she'd wanted, right? To disabuse him of any ideas that the two of them were back on the path to reconciliation. She shook her head, left with no answers—none she could admit to anyway.

God, she was still so angry with him. *Still* so angry, after all this time. He'd lost his temper, broken her heart and never tried to make it right. Now he was ready, and she was just supposed to come running? Familiar beeps began to echo through the house to signal a call coming in from the front desk.

"What?" Paula snapped out the greeting.

"Uh." The young woman hesitated a beat. "DA Starker? I have Mr. Brooks here to see you."

The man was a glutton for punishment, Paula surmised. Or maybe he just wanted the last word. He'd had an affinity for that, she recalled.

"Send him up," she instructed. Why not? She'd give him a few more parting shots. Then it would be as she'd said at the restaurant: she was done.

The elevator doors slid open quietly, but Paula thought she'd wait for them to close and envelop them in privacy before she laid into him.

Linus didn't wait. He left the elevator car with unwavering determination driving his steps. He didn't stop until her back was against the wall and her mouth was being crushed by his.

"Line—"

"Quiet." His tone was a growl, gravelly and resonant with emotion. His perfect teeth scraped the curve of her jaw and lower to nip the silken column of her neck and along her clavicle.

Whatever parting shots Paula had to offer faded into her subconscious. Her legs had turned to water and quivered so much that she feared her stiletto stems would soon give way beneath her.

There was no cause for concern there. Linus had already taken her off her feet to secure her between himself and the wall. Paula curled her fingers into his open collar. He'd removed his tie, leaving the shirt unbuttoned to just below his collarbone. The rest of the tailored dark suit remained intact.

Paula only had a moment to grasp the material before it was out of her reach. Linus was dragging his kiss lower. Again, she tried.

"Line—"

"I said quiet, Paula." His mouth was rooted to the tip of her breast, still concealed beneath her dress and underthings.

It didn't matter. He suckled hard and withdrew her moan with ease. Linus set her to her feet, and Paula had but a second or less to collect herself before he lifted her again. He'd found his way beneath her dress and cradled her bottom through the barrier of her hosiery.

By the time she'd realized his intentions, she was already on the floor. Linus took her down slowly, until she was on her back in the middle of the foyer. Just as she got used to her change in position, she heard the unmistakable rip and felt the chill from the flooring. It was confirmation that her pantyhose had been torn beyond repair, and her flesh was bare against the gray marble.

The sound of tearing delicates continued until her panties were all that remained. Paula's gasp was underscored by a heavy sob when Linus used his thumb to work her through the crotch of the cottony fabric. Her lashes refused to be still; desire commanded them.

"Linus, my—my bed—"

"I'm not staying." With that, he sealed his mouth over her middle and sucked.

Paula arched into a perfect bow while her hands came to rest against the top of his head. She luxuriated in the soft ebony waves she found there and bit her lip to stifle further outbursts of her approval.

There was little hope of keeping that control as the assault continued. Her panties were soaked by need and Linus's kisses. Paula wanted out of them, and he let her squirm against the discomfort for only a moment before relieving her of the garment.

Again, his wide palms cradled her bottom en route to cupping her thighs, positioning them to his satisfaction. He took her then, tongue plunging relentlessly deep and with sheer possession. Paula instinctively tried to lift off the floor, but his hold was sure and it kept her pinned. Hungrily, her intimate muscles squeezed his gifted tongue in a welcoming embrace. Her thin heels were practically shrouded in the torn hosiery. Intermittently, they tapped in a makeshift rhythm, as if keeping time with every erotic plunge of his tongue. Her hands had turned as weak as her legs and lay palms up on the glossy floor. Her lips were parted and slack, allowing just the faintest sounds of pleasure to escape. Ravenous, low octave sounds vibrated from Linus's throat. He provided her pleasure and received much in return.

Paula's small gasps and moans, her hands open and accepting on the floor, the way she squeezed his tongue while he had his way inside her…it all combined to provide an unmatched delight. Linus withdrew every so often to suck and nip at her folds. He smiled, seeing the flesh contract and release in anticipation. His tongue made a trip around her clit, and Paula wriggled amid his unbreakable grip. He offered her no mercy—no reprieve—and paired the rotations with airy suckles as the nub grew even firmer against his tongue.

She was close, he could tell, and commenced a new torment to carry her over. His tongue penetrated deep, and he felt the flood of her need against it. Thick and creamy white, it coated his tongue and he was insatiable for it. Her breathing became a rapid chorus of pants that filled the space and told him she was in the throes of a powerful orgasm. He remained relentless in the pleasure he subjected her to. He thrust and circled his tongue with a determination that was shocking in its intensity.

Furrows formed between Linus's long, sleek brows as he fixated on drinking Paula in until her shudders subsided and he could no longer feel her coming. When she seemed to calm down, he withdrew slowly to apply damp kisses to her clit, the petals of her sex and her inner thighs.

Her discarded panties lay a few inches away. Linus reached for them as he pushed off his stomach to look down at her. When her bright eyes met his darker ones, he used the lingerie to wipe her from his mouth. His smile was seductively wicked when she rolled her eyes. To add fuel to the fire still raging unseen around them, he leaned close to drop a sweet kiss to her ear.

"I know you started that argument with me on purpose," he whispered.

Paula blinked, but made no move to face him…or to tell him he was right.

Linus wasn't looking for confirmation. He stood, pushing her panties into a front pocket inside his suit jacket. He favored her with a wink, while she watched him do it.

"I'm sorry I can't stay. Just wanted you to know there are no hard feelings." He gave a roguish smile and shrugged. "No hard feelings that'll mess with the sleeping arrangements, anyway. Let me know if you find anything on that drive," he said, as though they were simply wrapping up a meeting.

Paula guessed they were, in a way. She watched him fix his shirt cuffs and smooth a hand across the back of his head as he returned to the elevator at an easy pace.

The doors soon closed at his back, but Paula remained on her foyer floor for a long while.

Chapter 7

Outside Nassau, The Bahamas
One Week Later

The travelers had emerged victorious over the series of scheduling upsets they'd all encountered in preparation for the two-week getaway.

The cocktail hour aboard the luxury yacht, *Idella*, was livened up by an array of scheduling stories a few chose to share regarding their close calls with defeat. The details of the trip had unexpectedly shifted and caused the group to push up its timetable.

"I'm just gonna go ahead and put it out there that the travel gods are taking issue with us seeking sun and fun."

Tigo's comment drew laughter as well as agreement.

No one had forgotten all the frenzy associated with his and Sophia's wedding.

"Maybe it's a sign that we need to plan better, or else we're asking for trouble doing things at the last minute," said Clarissa.

"Come on, Clari." Rayelle Keats laughed at her best friend. "Are you really gonna stand there and call this trouble?"

There was more laughter, including Clarissa's. She tilted her glass in approval of Ray's remark.

The group had arrived from Philadelphia around 6:45 p.m. Once the *Idella* was en route to the villa, the golden time of day was upon them. Everyone had gathered on the hardwood sun deck for the sunset. The spot was furnished by a series of twin-sized chaises and cozy scoop chairs littered with cushiony, wine-colored throw pillows. The space curved into a wide, circular area lined with built-in sectionals littered with their own abundance of pillows. A small two-person Jacuzzi topped off the inviting nook. Eli, Clarissa, Tigo, Sophie, Rook and Viva were in the midst of a heated debate over who got first dibs.

While the couples had opted for cozier chaise seating, Ray and Paula lounged on one of the built-in sectionals. So did Linus and Barker. The two men enjoyed their beer and talked politics and sports. Meanwhile, Paula and Ray watched the Atlantic zip by beneath steadily dimming skies.

"Was that a tone I heard or just my imagination?" Paula grinned, remarking on Ray's sigh.

"A tone? 'Course not."

The response drew quick laughter from Paula. "Come on now, it's not so bad…or is it?"

Rayelle snorted. "I wonder why the first thing a woman tries to do when she falls in love is see that all her friends do too."

A sultry smile curved Paula's mouth. "In the case of your friend, I have to say she's no slouch in the match-making department."

Ray slid a sly glance across the deck to where Linus and Barker were embroiled in a fierce discussion over the current NFL season.

"He is quite…something, isn't he?" Ray noted.

Paula tilted her head in acknowledgment. "Agreed," she said.

"And then there's Linus. Talk about *something*." Ray noticed the stunned look Paula sent her then.

"How do you know Linus is for me?" Paula demanded.

Ray replied at first with a lazy shrug. "Well…there *is* the fact that Sophia told me," she admitted, which Paula confirmed with laughter.

"Then there's the fact that Linus Brooks watches you like he wants to devour you."

Paula muttered a sudden curse as a vivid image flashed of her on the floor of her foyer with Linus Brooks doing precisely that. Determinedly, she willed the image to ease its torture.

"He seems like the kind of man who could hide a thing like that if he wanted to," Ray went on. "And it doesn't seem like he wants to," she finished.

"No…no he doesn't." Paula left the sectional and

went to study the view from the chrome railing that outlined the luxury boat.

Ray joined her there. "History?" she guessed.

"Mmm…a bad one," Paula shared.

Ray smiled. "That can't be totally true. In your best friend's defense, she's no slouch in the matchmaking department either."

Paula shook her head. "Linus and me, we…we're different people now. There're just some things you can't go back to."

"Is there still love there?"

"Why?"

Ray shrugged. "Nothing…maybe it's that you *won't* go back instead of *can't* go back."

"So?" Paula felt herself bristling.

"Wouldn't is final. Couldn't…there's the chance that things may change."

Paula arched a brow in Ray's direction. "You sure you don't have a law degree hanging in your office?"

Ray laughed. "Quite sure!"

"There are some things that can't be fixed, Ray," Paula said, sobering. "Not even with love."

"Okay."

"Love's got no chance when communication's out of the picture." Paula knew she was trying to convince herself even as she spoke the words.

"So you're not talking to him?" Ray probed.

"I can't. Not about this. It's been too long, and being reminded of who I was then—" Paula stopped herself, waving a hand to signal she'd had enough.

"I get it, Paula, and I'm sorry for prying." Ray gave another shrug. "Hazard of the job I guess."

Paula laughed then. "Mine too. Tell me, do you think there are some memories that are worth trying to fix so they end better when you remember them?"

Again, Ray shrugged. "I can't think of any memories I have worth digging up to fix. Guess in the end, you have to weigh the strength of the memory."

Paula smiled. "I take back what I said about the law degree—a psychology degree is what you should have."

There was laughter before quiet settled over them. It covered the entire deck as everyone focused on the horizon. There, the sun began its descent behind the waves. It was truly a glorious sight, made more spectacular by the anticipation of the days of relaxation that stretched before them.

"Cap estimates we should be there within the hour." Eli's voice surged resonantly across the deck once the setting concluded.

"He suggested we spend the rest of the trip on the bridge deck. We could have drinks around the fire," he continued. "With the sun down, the chill's gonna set in quick."

Rook Lourdess stood suddenly and hoisted his fiancée over his shoulder. "I like the way you think, man."

"Damn right," Tigo agreed, standing as well to cart away his wife.

The sun deck gradually cleared. Paula remained, wanting a few extra minutes to enjoy the unmatched view of the skies. The space was brilliant, with a colorful mix of reds, blues and purples. Even amidst the darkening skies, the waters were still a vibrant cerulean blue. She only wanted time alone to send up a fast prayer for strength and diplomacy over the next couple of weeks. If Linus planned to rile her with his incessant staring and smoldering...everything...she was going to need every drop of strength and diplomacy she could muster. Not only muster, but then hang on to. It was all too clear that her willpower stores were pitifully bare when it came to him.

At least there was still the Miranda Bormann issue to be solved. There had been no new developments, but Paula had to admit that she was enjoying getting her hands into another mystery. In her current position, such tasks were in the hands of her staff.

She was pretty much set on the plan to step away from the DA's office. Until now, she hadn't been so set on what her next move would be once the big desk was in her rearview.

Miranda Bormann's curious situation had helped remove those blinders and given her the clarity required to navigate the next chapter of her life. Taking on cases of her choosing, bypassing public scrutiny over those choices—to an extent—yes, that appealed to her greatly.

And beyond that? Would she be content with only her career? She was sure her life would be a fulfilling one, but would it compare to what she'd pretty much turned her back on since she and Linus had parted ways? Love and forever weren't in the cards for her and any man—unless he was Linus Brooks. Unfortunately, *the man* couldn't be Linus Brooks.

Talk to him...

Paula squeezed her eyes shut and decided she'd had enough of the view. Linus apparently had not. He was there when she stepped back from the rail. There was no mistaking that it was his frame crowding her.

"It's all yours." She sighed, still trying to back away.

But he wouldn't allow it. "Is it?" he murmured, lips close to her ear before he applied a faint suckle.

Paula tried to disentangle herself, but Linus held her fast.

"How's your—your staff coming along with the investigation?" she asked, hoping to put things on a track she could handle. "Have they found anything to connect your projects to Hayden Bormann?"

"Not yet." Linus's attention to her ear cooled. "I hope it stays that way. Doesn't sit well with me or my partners, thinking we could be involved in something like this. Have you talked to Miranda Bormann? Does she have anything more to add besides what was in that dossier you left with me?"

Paula moved closer to the railing, taking delight in the sea air hitting her face. "She thinks she might have something that could show Hayden Bormann's suspected clients that he's dealing falsely with them."

"Like evidence?" Linus watched Paula shrug her confirmation.

"Just speculation on her part for now. She'll send me whatever else she finds, and we'll go from there afterward."

Silence held for several minutes, and then Paula was easing back from the rail, once again trying to distance herself.

Once again, Linus wouldn't allow it. "It wasn't about you, Paula."

She inhaled sharply. His words stilled her more effectively than a physical embrace ever could.

Linus shifted then, leaning against the rail to watch her. "That night wasn't about you," he said. "What I did—it wasn't directed at—at you. I…you don't have any reason to believe me when I tell you I never would've tried to hurt you that way."

"I know that, L. I know you wouldn't have resorted to violence no matter what you…found out."

"I didn't give a damn about what I found out, Paula." He left the rail to crowd her against it once more. "What I found out couldn't have mattered less to me."

"But you said—"

"You knew I had money—that I came from money." He grimaced as though he despised the fact. "Some people with money get very paranoid over new people trying to enter their world."

"I didn't want your money."

"My brother didn't care that you didn't. He wanted you gone and did what he could to make that happen. He succeeded."

"Your brother." Her tone was a whisper. "You never said—"

"Because I hadn't seen him in six years. He picked that night to show up with that report on you."

Paula smiled. "Didn't think I was that important."

"You were going to be my wife. You were important, alright." He smoothed a hand over his jaw and sighed. "Our grandmother had passed away. She left me everything."

Understanding crept into Paula's light eyes. "A new wife might have taken your brother's seat on the gravy train."

It was Linus's turn to smile. "Somethin' like that."

"That's it?" Paula tilted her head. "There's nothing else to the story?"

"Nothing that matters," he countered without hesitation. "What I said, Paula. It was—I was never angry with you. That emotion was all for my brother and you—you just happened to be the unlucky recipient."

Paula nodded, inwardly telling herself to stifle the flurry of questions that had lain dormant for so long. She couldn't quite manage it.

"Is your brother older or younger?"

"Older." Linus didn't seem to understand the simple query. "Why?"

Paula gave a curious smile. "Just interesting that your grandmother would leave everything to you—guess your brother's paranoia set her on edge too."

"Somethin' like that." Linus reiterated his earlier response. Then he shook his head as if to clear it. "I just needed you to know."

"And that's all I need to know?"

"As far as that's concerned, yes."

Accepting, Paula nodded and prepared to move past him. Linus prevented the move one final time.

"As far as *we're* concerned," he said, "you should know I don't plan to lose you again."

"Linus, we can't—"

"We have. We will." He sealed the space remaining between them and left her no room to retreat. "I think you know I don't mind pressing an issue if I have to." He left the soft threat lingering on the air, kissed Paula's neck and left her alone on the deck.

Forty minutes later, the group had returned to the sun deck. The spot was the best place to observe their approach to the island. Claudette's Key was less than ten miles off the coast of Finley Cay, another island that rested along the chain of uncharted destinations amid the tropical waters of The Bahamas.

From the deck, the villa appeared a gleaming oasis in the middle of nowhere. According to Eli, Tigo and Linus, the private island was said to be a botanical wonderland, home to an exquisite array of flora and fauna. Its bird species were said to be of particular beauty.

The birds were presumably tucked away in their nests when the *Idella* pulled into its slip at the villa's private deck. There was only the rustle of wind between the healthy leaves of towering palms that dotted the landscape. For a while, the travelers could only stand in awe of the night sky that appeared to mingle shades of dark blues and purples. The faint glow of lightning flickered behind low-hanging clouds. By contrast, a pool shimmered with emerald waters illuminated by submerged lighting. The pool encircled the entire villa and could be accessed from virtually anywhere.

The passengers disembarked and made their way down the long pier leading to their lodging for the two-week stay. The villa was a stunning work of wood, brick, stone and marble. Its Aztec themes were evident in the furnishings, statues and architecture. The design was airy with the fresh scent of sea and foliage circulating throughout. The villa exuded an exotic openness as well as a cozy warmth heightened by its color scheme of soothing tans, beiges, browns, golds and creams.

Everyone dispersed to take their own informal tours of the vast structure and to locate their quarters. The *Idella*'s crew would handle transporting baggage from the boat to the specific suites.

Paula counted herself among the lucky few when she arrived in the suite to find her luggage already waiting. Finding her things all accounted for, however, wasn't nearly as satisfying as her accommodations.

Via suite access, there was the option of taking a short flight of stone steps down to the pool or remaining on the private patio, where a two-person in-ground awaited. The small, square lounge pool sat beneath a vibrant palm and was shielded by waist-high hedges that opened out toward the endless waters.

After a full day of travel, Paula had decided to turn in early and rest up for the full day of sun and fun awaiting her tomorrow. She quickly reconsidered the idea.

No one had said a thing about her own private pool just a few steps outside her room. Sleep could wait. Sleep wasn't even on her radar. She rooted around inside one compartment of a large duffle until she found a two-piece to suit her needs. It didn't take long for her to strip off her travel clothes and slip into relaxation. That relaxation amplified when she settled into her pool to find the water soothingly heated. A built-in timer set the water to warm once the sun went down and the island was flooded with cooler night air.

The pool's interior was fashioned into makeshift seating that resembled armchairs. Relaxation indeed. Paula reclined and happily allowed the heat, fragrant air and captivating night sky to whisk her into oblivion.

It worked…for a while. Then she found her gaze drifting along the striking beachfront. The white sands appeared vivid under the cover of dark. The contrast made her think of Linus and how striking his body would appear against the gleaming beach. Moreover, she imagined what she would look like, *feel* like against him—against the gleaming beach.

Squeezing her eyes shut, she silently willed away the images. It was no use, of course. She'd been denied Linus Brooks's erotic skill for way too long. Now, she was suddenly privy to an abundance of it, and *willing it away* was an impossibility if there ever was one. With that in mind, Paula tried to wedge in additional ways to douse the intensity of those images. She recalled their conversation on the yacht. The fact that she'd been the target of an intense background check was almost as curious as the fact that Linus had never mentioned he had a sibling.

He'd given her no reason for the omission, but it was clear he and his brother weren't a close pair. Especially with their grandmother bypassing the elder brother in favor for the younger to stand as heir to her money. What was that about?

Nothing that matters, he'd said.

Nothing that matters, and yet he'd returned from

the meeting with a brother he'd never mentioned, and dissolved into a rage that had him tossing furniture around like it was paper. On top of that, he now had no intentions of serving up any kind of explanation. Some apology.

Paula pursed her lips over the annoying truth. They were almost married, for goodness's sake! She'd tried not to look too stricken when he'd said it earlier. She was sure she hadn't done the best job. How could she? He'd said it so matter-of-factly.

You were going to be my wife.

Of course she'd known, *hoped* they were heading that way. Hearing him say it though…confirming that he'd wanted the commitment too…it had almost stopped her heart.

His brother though…his brother had hated the idea of them. He'd hated it so much, he'd dug up every dark element of her past and compiled it all to turn Linus against her. But to what end? Sure, she and Linus had parted ways, but the relationship between the brothers remained torn. Linus was still the sole recipient of their grandmother's estate. The lawyer in her warned that whatever it was he wouldn't share was something she needed to know. He'd made it sound as though the rest of the story was separate, as if it had no bearing on them.

Paula knew better—just as she knew having the rest of the story was only important if she planned to give Linus the second chance he wanted.

He wanted? Didn't she want the same? The *girl* in her wanted it. Paula shook her head quickly while submerging her shoulders in the warm water. The *woman* wasn't interested. Peace. No risks. No heartache. Again, Paula grimaced, knowing full well that a life of security and peace was no guarantee of avoiding heartache.

She shivered beneath the steamy water then—not out of soothing comfort, but uncertainty. Before her frenzied thoughts waged more war on her mind, she made a hasty exit from the pool. Sleep had suddenly become the only idea she wanted to entertain. She crossed the stone patio and was already peeling away the bottom of the black-and-tan swimsuit. There was a lot to be said for the feeling of absolute privacy in and out of doors. She entered the suite, pulling away the suit's halter-style top. The room was aglow from the brass lanterns placed throughout the sizable space of light brick and rich wood.

The lanterns held fat, battery-powered candles that doused the area in gold. Paula let her top fall to the dark travertine floor as she crossed it on her way to the wide bed waiting in its alcove of cream-colored brick. Relishing her surroundings and the sheer decadence of the moment, she leaned on one of the huge beechwood columns that covered the room.

She rested her forearm against the column and studied the glorious bed. She debated then on giving Sophia a call to cancel meeting up with her in the morning. After breakfast, the girls were going to explore the various coves and bays in and around the island. The plan was to take a day cruise aboard the *Idella* until lunchtime. Still eyeing the bed, Paula was sure she'd only just be turning over around lunchtime.

Once again, sleep was the only thing on her radar, and once again sleep took a back seat. This time, the reason was for something even more delicious than enjoying her very own pool.

She moaned, the sound wavering and muffled against her forearm. "L," she sobbed.

"Shh…casy," he urged.

"How—" Paula winced, every part of her riddled with shivers of pleasure "—how'd you get in?"

Linus smirked even as he nipped her shoulder. "It's all in the wrist." Her flesh was still cool and damp from her dip in the pool. He provided an example of his words by driving his middle finger high into the gripping sheath of her core. The driving rotations joined the gentle brush of his thumb over her clit while his free hand clutched her thigh, keeping her spread for his play.

Paula clutched at the column, hugging it to her as she rocked back against Linus's unyielding frame. She relished the feel of his bare chest at her back. "You can't be here…" She bit her lip as renewed sensation claimed her.

Linus chuckled. "Guess you should've packed your security."

"I'm capable—" she managed the boast amid a sharp gasp "—capable of handling unwanted visitors."

"Unwanted, huh?" He smiled as her moisture coated his fingers. "Doesn't feel like that pertains to me." To emphasize his point, he transferred her creamy need from his fingers to her thigh and filled her with his middle fingers until she stood on her toes and cried out her approval.

It was no surprise that he knew just how far to drive

her before she reached that final elated peak. Paula moaned her disapproval when she felt the delicious pressure ease. Linus took her with only one finger then while pulling a condom from the back of his denim shorts and tearing into it with his teeth. Soon after, the denim pooled at his ankles. He wore nothing beneath, and smoothly set the protection in place.

Paula barely had time to register the fact that he was as naked as she. Moreover, he was dark and chiseled, like something untamed and lethal. Again, his fingers were at her sex. With sultry expertise, they massaged her honey-toned folds before he palmed her upper thighs and spread them to accommodate his thick erection. It nudged her bottom before smoothly occupying the portal it sought.

Paula hugged the column ever more tightly, as eager for release as she was for the prolonged pleasure he was so capable of. Relentlessly, his hips slammed against hers. Pumping his shaft deep, he stretched her deliciously and coaxed an orgasm-inducing pleasure that Paula was all too eager to welcome.

Unfortunately, Linus was ahead of her on that score. He'd come there that night intent on being selfish and driven to take what he wanted, and then leave her unsatisfied and feverish for him. He wanted her to need him until she couldn't think—until all she cared about was having him. All else would be secondary, unimportant. She wouldn't care about the past then, and he could have her back without ever sharing the complete and humiliating story behind his loss of control.

Hungrily, his hands roamed her body, squeezing her

hips before cupping her belly and then her breasts. He fondled them mercilessly until her head tipped back to bring her earlobe within reach of his seeking lips. He sucked the plump lobe hard and ravenously while claiming her with ever-more-vigorous strokes that took him to the brink and pushed him over.

Linus clutched the column then too, having traded his fondling grasp on her breast for it. He erupted, strongly and generously. Paula released a throaty gasp when the heavy surge of his seed met the condom's thin casing. Linus savored every aspect of his climax, even the sweet squeeze of her intimate muscles around his shaft. She was still in the throes of being pleasured—not quite ready to ascend to her own peak just then.

Linus didn't plan on giving her the chance. Her next gasp was mixed with surprise and confusion when she felt him leave her.

"Linus?" She turned to find him fixing his shorts.

"Miss me," he simply commanded. Following a kiss to her jaw, he left her at the column where he'd found her.

Chapter 8

"Bitches," Paula seethed when she arrived at the dock the next morning. Despite her certainty that she'd still be snuggled in bed at that time, she had experienced just the opposite. No surprise, given her state of mind when she'd hit the sheets.

It had been hours before she'd finally drifted off. When she had, her slumber had been a restless one. She had been barely unconscious, her body still uncomfortably hot and aching with unsatisfied need.

"Damn him," she said of Linus as she watched the yacht getting smaller as it cruised deeper into the bay without her. The girls had made plans for a day of sightseeing. Though she'd been uncertain about joining in, Linus's impromptu visit the night before had quickly changed her mind. What happened had been no accident. He'd come to her room with plans to accomplish precisely what he had. He'd satisfied himself and left her unfulfilled and craving more.

She'd wanted more. How she'd wanted more. Something else weighed in over her physical wants, however. She wanted the explanation he hadn't seemed ready to fully provide.

"Ready." She considered the word.

Ready indicated it was only a matter of time. Linus's words indicated that the time would never arrive. That was good, wasn't it? She didn't want the full truth, did she? She thought she didn't before…and now—

"Tough break."

Paula whirled to find Linus standing just a few feet behind her. His molten chocolate stare appeared more vibrant against the tropical morning sun as he too stared at the *Idella* disappearing around a bend in the bay.

"Guess they thought you wouldn't make it," he said.

"Wonder what would've given them that idea?"

Linus barely shrugged in response. Paula rolled her eyes as she resumed her study of the quiet waters.

"If you're bummed about it," he said, moving closer, "I'm sure we could arrange something."

The offer made Paula smile. "I'm sure we could." She averted her face so he couldn't see her lashes flutter when he moved close to cup her hips.

"I'm not going to bed with you, L." She swallowed around the ball of need, suddenly occupying her throat.

"That's the great thing about a place like this." He didn't seem discouraged by her decision. "There are all sorts of places we could substitute for a bed."

Paula resisted letting her head fall back to his shoulder when his fingers found their way beneath the short wrap skirt that shielded her bikini. He began to stroke the crotch of the shimmering lavender material, and the swollen needy flesh beneath all but screamed for more. Still, she resisted. Her stubbornness refused to let him have his way.

"Don't." She felt the faint tremors from his body against hers when he chuckled.

"Alright."

He stopped, and Paula felt like she'd been left to drop to the ground without a parachute. His intention wasn't to leave her quite so coldly though. Hands at her waist again, he turned her to face him and took her mouth before she could think to verbalize a response.

Paula knew her only response would've been to tell him to give her more. Need had her gripping his T-shirt as the material rippled gently against the breeze. His tongue launched a possessive invasion, sliding, exploring, occupying every hidden crevice of her mouth. She reciprocated the erotic act. Fingers curling more tightly into his shirt, she drew him closer. She only needed to balance slightly on her toes to comfortably reach his mouth. Linus made it even easier for her, firming up his hold at her hips to hoist her higher against his tall frame.

Warning bells sounded in the far corners of Paula's mind, telling her that this moment had the makings of an ending with her still writhing, unsatisfied and pleasure-stricken. A few more encounters like the one last night, and she'd be little more than a mindless walking shell.

The distinctive pop and clatter of a bottle cap hit the

air. The sound served to anchor Paula to her sanity as she recognized the notification chime from her phone. She broke the kiss, thankful for the excuse to do so. If not for the warning alarm, she would've allowed the embrace to draw her deeper into desire's abyss, whether satisfaction awaited her there or not.

"My phone." She was already reaching for the device tucked into a hidden pocket along her skirt. Linus eased his grip and let her slide down the length of him. Paula turned to check the notification that could've waited.

She'd left her business phone in the suite. Her staff knew to only contact her personal line if there was a real emergency. The notification was from Miranda Bormann; it was an email with an attachment.

"Looks like you were right," she told Linus once she'd reviewed the brief message with the vague subject line entitled PART 1. More to come, was all the message read.

"JPEGs," she announced, noting the large file attachment of photographs.

"The evidence she spoke of," Linus added.

"Looks like it," Paula confirmed, still frowning over the images she studied. "Guess I would've had to cancel with Sophie after all." She sent Linus a resigned smile. "I think I should talk to your partners, unless you've all got other plans?"

Linus commended himself on keeping his bristling veiled. He'd worked closely with Sophia and the others to square away time with Paula during the trip. Of course, everyone was delighted to help, but Linus had overlooked the wild card in the plan: the situation with Miranda Bormann.

He'd been an idiot to think it wouldn't follow them there. He'd known it would. Whatever the mystery, it needed to be solved. None of this sat well with him, Eli or Tig, to know such a shadow loomed over their business. Nevertheless, his time with Paula was precious to him. When he returned to Philadelphia, he wanted Paula Starker on his arm the way she should've always been.

"Linus?" Paula was watching him expectantly.

"What do you need?" He gave himself a mental shake.

"Thirty minutes, forty-five at the most," she said. "The file's pretty large. We won't get through it all in one sitting, but since there's more to come and this is only part one, we should delve in as soon as possible." She shrugged then and gave another look toward the phone. "Maybe we'll get lucky with this first batch and come across a project that matches one of yours."

Linus couldn't deny the plan's logic. Besides, Eli and Tig had already reserved the day to get a little work done anyway. The info he'd already shared with Paula via the flash drive was supplied with a healthy stash of images. Of course, they were of little use without an anchor. Finding a match in Miranda Bormann's files could be the break they needed.

With any luck, they might actually solve the mystery sooner rather than later. That bit of luck would leave him the chance to focus on how he really wanted to be spending his time.

"L?"

He hedged then, somewhat annoyed by her eagerness to work and his lingering eagerness to play.

"It's kind of short notice, Paula."

"Is that right?" Her gaze narrowed and her smile was playfully wicked once the distance between them closed. She patted his cheek, refusing to be sidetracked by how flawless his skin felt next to her palm. "I'm sure we can arrange something."

Linus acknowledged her play on his earlier words. Paula left him with a smile before she sauntered off.

"Going the wrong way on a day like this, aren't you?"

Paula slowed her stride toward the cabana, where she'd been asked to meet with the Joss partners later that morning.

"Off the record?" she asked Barker, whom she had met as he was on his way down the stone walkway leading to the beach.

Barker pretended to be offended. "We just spent the night under the same roof. Surely we can both be trusted?"

Paula laughed. "Well, I'm still sorry for ruining your guys' day."

"Aw." Barker waved her apology away. "It was just gonna be me and Rook for most of it anyway. We're going into Nassau to scout clubs for later." He waved again, that time toward a sleek dark speedboat waiting along the shore.

"Nice." Paula's smile was a knowing one. "The cushy life seems to agree with you. You should watch that, or it might try to hold on to you."

Barker's smile turned dry, his dark stare scanning the shoreline. "Looks like the powers-that-be are already trying to make that a reality."

"Sounds mysterious. Are the powers-that-be your employers? Are the rumors going around true?"

Barker grinned, casting his gaze to the ground momentarily. "Off the record, Madam Prosecutor?"

"Of course."

Barker's grin grew wider. "They're trying to get me to take a desk job."

"Right." Paula nodded. "I heard the new chair of WPXI's programming board was trying to shake things up over there."

Barker didn't look too pleased by the tip.

Paula read his expression easily. "You should be honored and excited, you know? In the driver's seat, you could get some real information flowing to the people that certain powers-that-be might prefer to remain hidden."

"Or it could just be an elaborate way of distracting me from a story that they would prefer remain hidden."

A measure of seriousness took its place in Paula's eyes. "Is there anything my office needs to know?"

"In time." Barker folded his arms over his chest. "Right now, I'm just trying to get folks to talk to me."

"And are these 'folks' suspected of criminal activity?" Paula put her Joss meeting concerns to the back burner.

Barker shook his head. "But there's a chance they know things it'd be smarter to keep quiet about." Again, he shook his head as though to clear it. "Didn't mean to hold your ears hostage, DA Starker. Thanks for listening, and I promise to clue you in when the time is right."

"Don't take too long, alright? I'm about to vacate my seat and I can't promise that my successor will be as helpful."

"What was it you said about rumors being true?" Barker seemed newly engaged in the conversation.

"Off the record, Mr. Grant?"

Barker chuckled. "We're gonna have to work on our trust issues."

Laughter surged on both sides then. Soon though, Barker was nodding toward the cabana.

"Have fun in there," he said. "They don't seem too happy today."

"Yeah." Paula studied the cabana as well. "I kind of figured that."

"How much access does her nephew have to her assets?" Eli asked while the slide show played out on the room's far wall.

The beach cabana was located a short walk from the villa. A sturdy Spanish tiled roof topped a spacious stone structure that consisted of one room that accommodated a kitchen, bath area and sunken seating that faced the beach. A drop-down viewing screen could be activated by remote. It blocked a portion of the area and was handy for an entertaining night in or out of doors. Yet the stone-faced group seated before it didn't appear at all entertained.

Paula had logged into the cabana's Wi-Fi from her phone and opened Miranda Bormann's email in order to view the JPEGs via the screen. She, Eli, Linus and Santigo had been reviewing the images for the past ten minutes. This followed a brief chat regarding the projects that had so far captured their attention.

"According to Miranda Bormann," Paula told Eli, "her nephew's had his hands in every part of this, which is why she was hesitant to go to anyone else in the family."

"And this is part one," Tig noted, "of Henry Bormann's vast holdings. It stands to reason that Hayden Bormann would think he could make moves and go unnoticed."

"He still took enough precautions to make sure his visits went unnoticed, right?" Linus asked Paula.

She nodded. "The PI Professor Bormann hired found no evidence—at least photographic evidence—of him meeting with anyone they could label as a client except Joss. You in particular," she said to Linus.

"It was dumb luck the PI tailed Bormann going into Joss," she added. "The fact that you're the guy to see puts you in the hot seat, I'm afraid."

Appearing to consider that, Linus pushed up from the oversized snow-white sectional that claimed most of the room and surrounded a wide, glass coffee table.

Paula guessed she'd said enough and began to collect her things. "I forwarded the attachment to you all. If anything looks strange, we can discuss it. I talked to Professor Bormann this morning, and she's got the PI's staff scanning the photos as fast as she can uncover them."

"And what are these again?" Eli asked.

"Boxes of old family photos. Some of them are of places the Bormanns would meet for family gatherings. Professor Bormann's husband was real big on them being a tight-knit group."

Tig snorted. "That can be hard to do when there's money like this involved."

Linus's heavy sigh caught everyone's ear. The sound mixed with something that carried an unmistakable guttural noise. Eli and Tig traded looks. They knew very well the kinds of displays that tended to follow that sound.

"Thanks, Paula," Tig said.

Paula nodded and made her way from the room.

"Alright, man?" Eli asked before nodding in reply. "Dumb question," he noted at the fierce look Linus gave him.

"Why don't you just go after her already?" Tig huffed.

"It's not that easy, especially now, especially with this." Linus waved toward the slide show of images still playing on the screen.

"Hell, Line, Paula isn't accusing you of anything," Eli argued. "We're just the only lead Miranda Bormann's detectives have so far."

"That's not it, E." Linus began to pace in the confined space. "She knows I'm keeping something from her."

"This is about what happened between you guys before," Tig said.

"But you already talked to her about that," Eli added.

"I told her what happened wasn't about her, that I wasn't angry—not with her," Linus clarified.

"And she didn't believe you."

"I think she did," Linus said to Tig's guess and then muttered a curse while smoothing both hands over his head. "She's so damned smart," he added as though it pained him to admit the fact.

"She thinks there's more to the story." Eli guessed that time.

"Is she right?" Tig watched Linus nod and then shrug.

"I can't tell her," he admitted.

"Isn't that why you brought her here?" Eli queried. "To tell her everything and get you back on track?"

"It's not that easy with us, but yeah, that was part of the plan. I, um, I couldn't make myself go there, you know? Even in memory, I couldn't."

"So what's your plan then? Since I know you don't plan on goin' back to Philly without her on your arm," Tig challenged.

At first, Linus only shook his head. "It might come down to me doing that very thing—all depends on how this turns out."

"Listen to me, Line. I don't care if we all had a four-course meal with Hayden Bormann, it doesn't make us crooks." Eli's handsome face was a closed, dark mask. "We don't run our business that way. Whatever this is, we aren't involved."

"I get that, E. I do." Linus reclaimed his seat to study the images still flashing across the screen. "Something about this won't let go. I don't know how, but I got the feeling we're very much involved in this."

Eli and Tig traded looks again. They knew better than to argue with each other's instincts. Their business had thrived because they trusted each other's gut feelings.

"So are you just gonna give up?" Tig smiled at the look he got from Linus.

"If it wasn't for that damn phone of hers this morning, we'd be spending the day together right now," Linus shared. "That email from Miranda Bormann came in before I could get her out of there."

Tig grinned. "You know how to fix that, don't you?"

"Damn right I do. Next time, I won't give her time to prepare."

"You know she's too smart to let this go," Eli pointed out. "Time alone with her means more time for her to question you about what you're keeping."

"Exactly," Tig agreed. "She's a prosecutor, and a damn good one. When it comes right down to it, you're gonna have to revisit this thing—to look it straight in the eye and confront it."

"And you two really think this is a good idea?" Linus smirked. "Confronting this thing while I'm alone with her?"

"You didn't hurt her then. You won't now."

"E's right. You've fought this too hard and too long to let it win now when you finally have another chance."

"At least tell her how difficult this is for you to talk about, man," Eli suggested.

"Weak." Linus spoke the word as if it were a curse.

Eli and Tig traded looks for the third time that morning. Another thing they knew all too well about their friend was that he loathed appearing weak. For the last several years, that hatred had manifested in his passion to make Joss Construction a recognizable force. The endeavor turned out to be a healthy outlet for the final remnants of the rage that drove him. Eli and Tig were no fools; they knew it would only be a matter of time before substituting his passion for strengthening their business lost its power over an avoidance to be seen as weak.

"Do you love her?" Tig asked.

Linus rolled his eyes. "'Course I do."

"Then if there's anyone you shouldn't give a damn about seeing you at your weakest, it's her."

Linus shook his head at Tig's reasoning. "You don't know where she came from—the way she grew up. She's known enough weak men in her life."

"And how would you categorize a man who lies to the woman he loves?"

Linus waved off Eli's notion. "You don't know what you're talking about. No offense, E, but you and Clarissa have no history."

"Soph and I do," Tig chimed in. "Good luck getting Paula all the way back if you don't plan to be all the way truthful with her."

A smidge cocky then, Linus shrugged. "She loves me, wants me. That hasn't changed. All I have to do is—"

"What? Make love to her until she follows you anywhere? Forgets all the questions floating around in her head about you?" Tig grinned. "That ain't happenin', brotha."

"I know what I'm doing."

"Hell, man, do you really think that'd work?" Tig laughed.

“Save it, T. Tell me you didn’t try that with Sophie.”

“Tried and failed. I’d like it if you and Paula didn’t have to go through the drama maze we did.”

Linus took pity then. “I appreciate the concern from both of you and I agree. She’s no idiot, and definitely not a woman who’d have her mind go blank after a few hours in bed. If I can’t make things right with her, I’ll damn well enjoy the time I have with her while I have it.”

“And what if she wants to enjoy her time with you doing more than making love under the stars?” Eli probed. “She already knows there’s more to the story than you told her. She may want your pillow talk to be a little more substantial. What then? You say you love her. Are you willing to put what she needs over what you want?”

Linus considered the questions his friends posed. But instead of answering, he left the room.

Chapter 9

Spirits had lifted tremendously by the time the dinner hour arrived. The group met in a dining room fit for gods or, at the very least, kings. The area occupied a vast space along the villa's multilevel rooftop. It overlooked the bay that mirrored the pastel blue shades of the late evening skies above.

A steady, comfortable breeze kept the palm leaves and flowers swaying actively amid aromatic air that swept the open construction of wood and stone. Darker wood composed the high ceiling that was softly lit by a trio of low-hanging chandeliers. Electric candles gleamed behind a series of cylindrical tinted lanterns on the table. Hanging vines and bushes outlined a spot that was equipped with a stone hearth in the corner.

There, a fire blazed brilliantly to combat a chilly breeze blowing in off the surf.

Besides the hearth, diners had an unobstructed view of the bay and sky. The dining room's interior flooring was light brown stone. The heavy table was fashioned of rich wood with a distinctive charcoal-brown color. Wide wicker chairs accented the wood and stone color scheme. The diners held the same opinion that they were as comfortable as they appeared, with thick cushions covering the seats.

The table could serve twelve easily. There were ten for dinner that evening, however, and they'd arrived in a state of awe. The view was unmatched, and pretty damn close to indescribable. The setting sun shaded the sky and clouds with an array of pastels in blends that were impossible for a human to duplicate.

"The view alone is worth whatever Maxton would want to charge for a night here," Rook declared.

No one responded, but everyone agreed. Still rather dazed, they managed to take their places at the table already aglow from the fat candles under glass.

"Who keeps up a place like this?" Viva asked.

"Same folks who handle the yacht," Tig told his sister-in-law.

"Convenient," Clarissa noted.

"Mmm…and another way to up the price," Sophia added.

"Have the owners mentioned what a night might go for?" Rayelle asked.

"Brace yourself," Eli said, then grinned. "Initial figures are being thrown around in the range of $25-$40K a night."

A round of hushed and shocked curses carried around the table.

"The price is why we're here," Linus chimed in. "To brainstorm ways to make it worth the expense."

"I agree with Rook." Paula shivered in approval of her surroundings. "The view alone goes a long way. Joss won't have far to go with a head start like that."

Low laughter surrounded the table, and shortly after, two uniformed servers arrived to begin filling everyone's water goblets and wine glasses. Paula, Clarissa and Sophie opted for wine. Rayelle, Viva and the guys chose from the array of beers on tap. The night's menu was to consist of hearty steaks, potatoes and homemade bread.

Linus took the liberty of ordering for Barker, who still had not arrived for dinner. Ray was first to notice his absence.

"He said something about having a conference call when we were out today," Rook explained.

"Oh yeah, you guys were scouting clubs," Paula mentioned.

For a while, the chatter fixed on that outing. Servers continued to mill about, supplying the night's appetizers. Fried asparagus chips with a gooey spinach and artichoke dip and wheat medallions with a seasoned olive oil were a few of the offerings.

"Everybody eat up," Rook advised. "Me and Bark found some dance halls guaranteed to work off every calorie you put on here tonight."

The laughter and conversation were still going strong when Barker arrived.

"Doesn't look like it was a fun chat with your colleagues," Tig noted.

"Yeah." Barker took his place at the table. "Others have been a lot more fun."

"Wanna talk about it?" Eli asked.

"*Can* you talk about it?" Viva queried playfully.

Barker laughed. "It's not top secret. Just a few of my reporters forgetting they're reporters and not interrogators."

"Ouch." Tig winced. "No fun when you've got to wear that particular management cap."

"No, it's not." Barker sighed. "But in their defense, they're a good group. A little green, so there's still some fine-tuning needed. A few who need to learn the difference between stressing to someone the importance of speaking out and berating them when they choose not to."

"Seems a lot of reporters could refine that skill, and not just the green ones," Rayelle decided.

"Some of your colleagues stress the public's right to know, and they forget the people they want to 'speak out' are a part of that public."

The group mulled over Sophia's valid point as the servers arrived with the meal. Mouthwatering aromas battled with the floral breeze to craft a fragrance that was nothing short of stellar. Conversations stalled hard and fast once the group dug in. The scrape of cutlery on the deep ceramic plates were the main sounds for a while. Quiet murmurs sifted around the table with requests to pass butter and sour cream for potatoes, steak sauce for the massive T-bones and New York strips. The meats had been grilled to perfection.

"Would I be off the mark to guess your reporters are having trouble getting witnesses to talk?" Ray asked when they'd been eating silently for a while.

"You wouldn't be off the mark at all." Barker grimaced with agreement.

Paula was grimacing then too. "I guess the words *rat* and *snitch* have been exchanged more than once."

"Yeah." Barker laughed shortly. "On several occasions."

"In situations like that, it can be impossible to get people to talk," Ray added.

"And I'm trying to get my people to see that not everyone trusts the press enough to open up, even if there's the possibility it could change their situation."

Barker's outlook drew a nod from Paula. "That's the problem right there. *Possibility*. Now, if we could talk guarantees…"

"Can't ever make those." Barker leaned back from the table as though he had no intention of eating any further.

"Until we can, your reporters are gonna have those difficulties all during their careers," Paula noted.

"You're in law enforcement, Paula," Rook chimed in. "Are you saying you approve of people not coming forward even for the mere possibility of things changing?"

"I think I'm saying I *understand* it, more than I approve of it." Paula outlined the mouth of her wineglass with her index finger. "Understanding why change isn't that grand a concept is a hard sell for people who grew up privileged."

"Ouch again." Tig swigged down what remained of his beer. He was provided with a full and chilled mug moments later.

"I'm not trying to step on toes, but when you grow up a certain way..."

"Underprivileged," Ray interjected and smiled.

Paula nodded. "It can be hard enough to believe a person means you well, and even harder to believe they can help you change your life."

"So I should tell my team to give up when it's clear they're dealing with things they don't understand."

"Giving up is the very last thing they should do, Barker." Paula was shaking her head then while sipping from the glass of Pinot Noir she'd requested. "But they need to exercise more patience and understanding. A person may be scared, but that doesn't mean they aren't willing to do what's needed to change their place in life. Tell them to keep trying, but gently."

"Thanks, Paula." Barker tipped his glass in toast.

Paula enjoyed another sip of her wine and found Linus's dark gaze on her when she set it down.

Enjoying more of the view was all anyone wanted to do once the filling meal had been finished. The view was a stunner by day or night, sunset or dawn. Still, none among the group could argue they weren't curious about what entertainment gems Rook and Barker had uncovered during their morning of club scouting. Besides, the steak dinner was more than deserving of being worked off at one of the shimmering dance halls they'd glimpsed upon arriving in Nassau.

They were ferried back by way of the *Idella.* Then they began their night of club hopping from the three horse-drawn carriages awaiting them at the pier. Rook and Viva occupied the only two-person carriage and brought up the rear behind the others. The city was a remarkable display of conversation, energy and lights that were just beginning to glow amid early evening skies. Women showed off ankle-breaking dance sandals while men were decked in their finest casual attire. In Nassau, club hopping was as much about fashion as it was about dancing.

The place was also about seduction. It hadn't escaped Paula that the night was also meant to entice. She and Rayelle had traded more than a few glances since they'd been seated in the comfortable white oak carriages. Ray and Barker rode in the first carriage, along with Clarissa and Eli. Paula and Linus had been tagged to ride along with Sophia and Tigo. All three of the loving couples were especially demonstrative that night. Paula was sure the underlying messages were meant for her and Rayelle.

Paula doubted those messages were meant for Barker, but she was sure Linus needed no prodding. He'd made a point of keeping his hands somewhere on her body since they'd boarded the *Idella.* Now, seated on the plush cushions across from Tig and Sophie, who kissed without any sense of propriety, Linus seemed intent on caressing Paula into the same state of wantonness. She wondered if he sensed that she was already there, and was sure he had. Clearing her throat, she tried to focus on a conversation that might take things in a direction opposite of where his hand on her thigh was trying to take it.

"Have you guys had any luck looking into those project links to Bormann? Does anything look familiar with the photo file I left with you earlier today?"

"I don't know. We didn't talk much about it when you left."

Paula shook her head as if she meant to clear it. The head shake though was mainly to dissuade his tempting mouth from the sensual glide it charted from her ear to the sensitive spot behind it. "Doesn't sound like much of a meeting," she said.

"Actually it was. My partners gave me some good advice." His words were a whisper as he returned to her ear and began a soft wet suckle of the lobe.

Paula felt like she was drowning and tried desperately to remain afloat. "So what was the advice?"

"Something like what you gave Bark. To keep trying and do so gently."

"Were they talking in terms of gratification?"

"Yeah, just a different kind."

"I thought we already covered that."

"Jeez, Paula, is sex all you think about?"

Her gaze flared as she sent him an incredulous look. Lips parted, she readied a retort that was cut silent when his tongue occupied her mouth. Paula felt more than heard the purr flooding her throat. Instinct had her thighs parting when his hand roamed higher, until his fingers were grazing her middle hidden beneath the jumpsuit she'd chosen for the night out.

His thumb mimicked the circular strokes of his tongue around hers. Paula rested on her willpower when her clit ignited under his tongue. She squeezed his wrist to still it.

Linus showed her mercy and eased off. But his features sharpened with a look that promised he wouldn't ease off for long.

The group had hopped around to three clubs, each more dazzling than the one before it. The architecture in connection with the breathtaking views made for several stunning establishments. Barker and Rook basked in the flattery from their companions over making such excellent selections. It was, however, the fourth selection that brought them the most praise.

The Star Gazer was a particular hot spot, and with good reason. The three-story club boasted circular balconies on either side that were dedicated dance floors, allowing visitors to lose themselves in music under the stars or amid the clouds when rain was in the forecast. The skies were star-filled that night, however, and club patrons took total advantage of the perfect weather.

Paula broke from the group shortly after they arrived. Eager to escape Linus's touch and her own lack of resistance to it, she headed off to shed her cares and concerns among the scores of bodies gyrating gleefully both in and outside the club's stone and tinted glass frame. She didn't remain unattached for long and found her escape in the arms of more than a few dance partners. She'd just taken the arm of one who offered to show her to the rooftop dance floor, when her arm was claimed by another.

"L—"

"Enough dancing."

Linus whisked Paula away so smoothly, she barely felt her hand slip from the elbow of the man escorting her.

"Linus." She was certain he couldn't hear her over the stirring roar of the music.

The Star Gazer offered dance alcoves for patrons who required more privacy for their movements. The spaces were numerous across the sizable club. Linus found one within moments of them stepping onto the second level.

"I thought you said 'enough dancing'?" she queried when her back bumped the alcove's padded black upholstered wall. Her lashes stirred when his voice hummed against her cheek.

"I did."

"Then why—?"

His tongue claimed her mouth for the second time that night. Unlike before, the claiming this time possessed a ruthless fervor. Paula didn't try to resist its tug on her every hormone. She met his seeking thrusts with lazier, contented ones of her own. She murmured a complaint when he halted the kiss to slide his mouth down her neck. She felt her feet leaving the thick, deep red carpeting of the alcove floor. Instinctively, her legs encircled his waist as Linus cupped and fondled her bottom. She could feel his lips retracing their heated path along her neck.

"Where was he taking you?"

Paula, becoming increasingly lost in the kiss, didn't answer. Linus ceased his nips along her neck and gave her bottom a decidedly firmer squeeze before he repeated himself.

"Wha-what?"

"Your partner?"

Awareness flooded Paula's gaze, but she maintained her bewilderment. "Which one?" She delighted in the shimmer of anger that was unleashed in his rich chocolate eyes.

"You shouldn't tease me."

"I thought you had a handle over letting your emotions control you?"

Linus's expression remained grim, though his voice harbored a noticeably lighter tone when he spoke. "My therapy didn't cover this part," he told her.

Paula rested back against the wall. "And exactly what is *this*?"

"I've never been jealous about you, Paula."

"That's commendable, considering there've been so many things to be jealous of over the years."

Linus shrugged and allowed his gaze to shift momentarily. "It's easier to deal with from a newspaper or through a TV screen. In person, though…" He shrugged again.

"I was just dancing with him—them," she clarified and his striking features sharpened. Then she laughed. "Are you really going to stand there and tell me you're jealous? From what I've heard, you could have your pick of over half the women in Philly to bring down here."

"Nice to know I've got the DA keeping such a good eye on me."

Paula rolled her eyes and tried to keep her mind off where his fingers were. "Doesn't take keeping an eye on you to do that," she said. "You know as many people as I do. Word travels…"

"None of them meant anything to me, Paula."

"And I do?" Her eyes narrowed and she nudged his chest with hers. "Don't worry about answering that. It's normal to let sex with an old flame screw with your head."

"She's only screwing with my head because I love her."

Paula bristled, knowing that an attempt to disentangle herself would be pointless. His hold accentuated a sensual delicateness, but Paula knew that was for form's sake. One move from her that he didn't care for, and that delicateness would easily flip to domination.

"Tell me you don't feel the same," he demanded before attempting to coax an answer out of her with a slow nibble of her earlobe.

When Paula refused to answer, Linus took his nibbling a step further. He supported her bottom fleetingly before his fingers grazed her middle.

"Tell me you don't, Paula."

"I'll do better than tell you." The longing coming from her eyes was replaced with accusation. "You don't love me, L. Not really. Not like you once did."

"How can you say that?" The sharp edge returned to his features.

"Seriously." Quiet laughter held the word. "We've been back in each other's lives all of a skinny minute. You can't feel the same, because back then you trusted me a helluva lot more than you do now." She gave the briefest of head shakes. "Of course, back then, you kept me in the dark too. Maybe if you hadn't, I wouldn't have been blindsided when I found you redecorating our room and accusing me of wanting to steal your piggy bank."

"I told you what that was about, P."

"But you haven't told me all of it. You say you love me, but you won't or can't trust me with the full truth."

"And do you really want that, Paula?" He allowed her to slide down him until her feet returned to the floor. "You really want to know my deepest and darkest parts? Really want to see what made me who I was then, and where it would take me to tell you about it now?"

Paula's expression changed as a more curious element crept into her gaze. "That's not who you are now."

"That's who I'll always be at the heart of it. We never lose who we really are, Paula."

"No, but we do learn how not to be defined by it."

"And what happens when I—what, Paula? Confess all to you?"

She shook her head again. "No idea. I want the entire truth, because you owe me that."

As though suddenly depleted, Linus braced his hands on the alcove wall and bowed his head. "The entire truth has nothing to do with you, Paula."

"And until you see what a load of crap that is, there's no hope for us."

"You mean, no hope until I strip myself bare for you? Let you see what I was—" He stopped, shut his eyes then. What he believed he could too easily be again if he opened that door… Linus considered the possibility in silence.

He didn't need to say more; she understood well enough. Whatever had happened between them—whatever hurts and guilt there were—it didn't touch the hurt and fear that his past held over him like a storm cloud. How the hell was she supposed to compete with that? How the hell did she convince a man like Linus Brooks that looking weak in front of her was the last thing he ever had to worry about? At any rate, *competing* with it was exactly what she'd have to do if she expected to get back the man she had never stopped loving.

"So we're done, is that what you're saying?" He knocked his fist against the wall and turned. "I screwed up again, didn't I?"

"No, L." Paula gave a sad smile. "You just pissed me off. I hear it's a pretty common thing when the folks involved are stubborn as mules."

Nodding, Linus rested back on the wall. "So what do we do about it?"

"No idea." Paula's sad smile carried a hopeful edge then.

"Do you want us back?" Linus pushed off the wall and then waved off the question. "Don't answer me. Just think about whether you do. Think about whether you can have us back only on your terms, because it may not be possible for me to meet them. I know what I want, Paula, and it's you."

He bristled then, as though he were bracing himself to move on to something he was reluctant to speak about. "I want you back, but not if it means you have to compromise yourself. If I'm not willing to do that, it's wrong for me to expect you to." Closing the small bit of space between them, he cupped her cheek. "I'm gonna get out of here. Let you enjoy yourself."

"Line—"

"I need to go, Paula." He fixed her with a crooked smile. "If I see you on the floor with some other fool, I'm sure to forget everything I've learned in my anger management classes." With those words, he kissed her cheek and left her.

Chapter 10

The group returned to the villa exhausted and eager for sleep. No one turned over until well past noon.

Paula was among the first out of bed. She wanted to check in with her office, as she'd been unfairly relying on her assistants to help with the planning for her annual holiday party. The event had become a tradition during her time in office and was always well attended. With all the legal drama in her office as of late, she hadn't had as much time to devote to the planning as she usually did. Paula was more determined to have the gathering that year, however. Given the decision she'd made to not seek reelection and to forgo public office for a more private one, her holiday gathering would be the perfect place to make that announcement.

After speaking with her office, she also took time

to contact Miranda Bormann to let her know there had been no new developments. Bormann didn't seem discouraged, and she told Paula she'd be sending a new file within a matter of hours. Following the call, Paula went to scrounge up a cup of coffee and was grateful to find several hot and cold beverage stations located throughout the immense villa.

The convenience saved her from running into Linus. Not that she'd have minded, only…she was still working to process all they'd discussed the night before. He still loved her, and she could admit how nice it was to know he'd never gotten over her just as she'd never gotten over him. He couldn't tolerate seeing her with other men—such an unnecessary thing for him to worry over. Still, it was nice to hear him admit it just the same. What did surprise her though and had her up and out of bed earlier than she otherwise would've been was hearing him tell her he was prepared to walk away if remaining together meant compromising herself.

It was the very last thing she'd expected to hear him say. It also underscored what she'd said about them being two people who were stubborn as mules. Mule-stubborn people didn't have the word *compromise* readily available in their vocabularies.

He'd acknowledged that, hadn't he? He'd said he wouldn't have her compromised if he wasn't prepared to be. She'd stewed over those words for the rest of the night and considered her uncompromising nature. It had served her well, but to what end? Sure, she had a stellar career, many accomplishments to speak of, a glamorous social life, blah-blah, but what of the things that mattered? The things that lasted? Things she'd once told herself were the true marks of accomplishment—family, love, commitment. She'd wanted those things with Linus once. When it all fell apart between them, she'd forced herself to accept that they weren't meant for her and most likely never had been.

Seeing Linus again now, being in such close quarters…she couldn't deny that she was lying to herself. She still wanted to achieve those true marks of accomplishment, still wanted the security of home and family, and she wanted it with Linus Brooks.

Linus didn't want her to compromise herself, but maybe that was exactly what she needed to do. Whatever it was that he wouldn't or couldn't tell her, it was a heavy weight. Clearly, it still had more of a hold on him than perhaps even he realized. He'd said it wasn't her that he had been angry with—that she was just… there. Should she let it go? Was the explanation worth demanding if it tortured him so to remember?

There was no time to answer the question in her head. Sophia's voice rang out.

"Hey, hey, hey! What are you still doing loafing around when a night cruise awaits us?"

"You can't be serious?" Paula gasped. "I figured this would be a night in after last night?"

Sophia flopped into a lounge chair and rolled her eyes as if to mourn her friend's lack of imagination. "Plenty of time for nights in when we're back in snowy Philly."

Paula only shook her head and sipped more tea. "So what's up today?"

"Oh, uh, it's better if you see for yourself, so start getting ready. We need to be at the yacht before sunset."

"Who's going?"

"Do you want to know who's going or who isn't?"

Paula set aside her tea. "You do know we're in or near international waters. I'm sure I could get away with any heinous acts I could come up with to take care of one of Philadelphia's finest."

"Oh, my friend!" Sophia's laughter was robust, her gray eyes alight with playful devilry. "I've only got evening yachting on the brain. I thought you might like to enjoy it with me and the girls since Linus has been keeping you all to himself lately."

"Mmm…and he's been doing that with a lot of help from you."

"I dare you to tell me you aren't enjoying it," Sophia all but purred.

"You remember we're here for business, right, Soph?"

Sophia sobered a bit. "Has anything broken with Miranda Bormann's case?"

"Not yet."

Sophia hiked a brow. "Should I take your tone to mean you think it will?"

"Sophie, I just don't want to get into something with Linus that I can't get out of."

"Ah, hon." Sophia sent her friend a pitiful look, leaned over from the lounge and smoothed a hand down Paula's cheek. "I'm afraid you're too late for that."

Linus hadn't left his suite all day. He'd gotten little in the way of sleep, but he rarely needed more than a few hours to be functional. Besides, he'd already gotten more than his fair share since they'd arrived in Claudette's Key. He'd devoted time to his portion of duties related to the proposed renovations. He'd also taken another look at the photo file Miranda Bormann had shared.

"There's probably nothing to it, Este. I just need to ease my curiosity, you know?"

"I'll get right on it Linus," Estella Mays promised her boss. "I hope you're at least spending as much time as you can having a *little* fun?"

Linus grinned. "Workin' on it, Este. Thanks." Ending the call, Linus thought over how he'd been spending his time. He hadn't spent nearly as much of it with Paula as he'd planned. Of course, as much as he'd planned was pretty much the equivalent of "all the time" so...

Linus grinned in spite of himself and the situation. He left the bed then, preferring a closer view of the calm sea. Standing before the early afternoon skies was just what he needed to soothe his busy mind. All night, he'd replayed the conversation with Paula—particularly his part of the conversation. The part he'd played in ruining them had been a bigger hurdle to climb than the drama that had ignited his anger in the first place.

Last night, he'd told her he was willing to walk away, and what the hell was that about? He finally had her back—sort of—after all this time, and he was offering to walk away? He was willing not to press her to give them another go? How many times in the past had the rage come over him precisely because he *had* walked away and not fought harder to keep her?

He wouldn't say he'd crossed any sort of bridge last night, but something had changed. Ironically, it reminded him of the lowest point in his life—one he'd give anything to forget. While he'd never put himself close to having the same level of tolerance to keep fighting as the woman who'd raised him, Linus believed he'd experienced a bit of that when he'd mentioned walking away.

Hard as it was, there was something soul-soothing about doing what needed to be done for the good of a loved one. Such was a core principle of what it meant to love unconditionally. Unconditional love was never a guarantee when it came to lovers, but was easily obtained between parents and children, or grandparents and grandchildren.

Linus squeezed his eyes shut to will away reminders of how that feeling had manifested in his grandmother's love for him…and his brother. She would have done anything for them because, for her, what mattered was the feeling that surged from doing what needed to be done for a loved one.

He wanted to clench a fist, but resisted the urge. He didn't want his brother's treachery justified. After all that had happened, all he'd lost because of it, he wasn't ready to be saddled with the chore of having to forgive the man.

But isn't that what you want from Paula? Her forgiveness?

Despising his train of thought, Linus slammed palm to fist and launched a determined pace around his patio. The soothing beauty of the late-afternoon skies was lost on him then, as was the desire to have company who would only be joining in on his grief. Linus heard the quiet rumble of laughter and knew that at least one of his friends had witnessed his display of frustration.

"Not in the mood." He barely glanced over his shoulder to speak to whomever it was.

"I disagree." Barker's voice resonated against the easy breeze. "Looks like you're in a helluva mood."

Linus gave in to the grin tugging at his mouth and turned to give Barker the full benefit of it.

In clear approval of the gesture, Barker took the rest of the steps up the side of the patio that led to the shore.

"So I'm in a bad mood." Linus conceded by spreading his hands slightly. "Why the hell aren't you in a worse one? All this beauty around us and there you stand—alone. Where's Ray?"

"Around." Barker laughed easily, but kept the gesture brief. "I was taking a call."

"Ouch." Linus made a face. "I thought Tig, Eli and I would be the only ones saddled with work during this trip. Looks like it's riding you the hardest though. What gives, man?" Again, Linus spread his hands. "As a loyal WPXI viewer, I believe I have a right to know."

Barker shared his grin again, but it was brief. "It's still a hush-hush deal, but they want me to pull back from some of my duties at the station. They want me to pull *all* the way back."

"They?" Linus prodded, nodding when Barker only stared. "Why? They've never interfered with your work before."

Barker shrugged. "I guess after all these years—all

the times I've refused when they've encouraged me to let stuff go—guess this time they've come across something they can't let slide."

"What the hell's goin' on, B?" Linus didn't mind showing his elevated concern. "The truth now, man. Is this about what you told us at dinner? Your reporters going over and beyond to get certain witnesses to talk?"

Barker nodded and went to perch along the cream stone ledge of the patio. There, he studied the foamy waves desperately trying to cling to the shoreline. "They're being more aggressive than usual, but that tends to happen when a boss they like starts getting death threats."

"Death threats? Bar—"

"Calm down, calm down." Barker waved off his friend's worry. "Do you know how often I have to deal with this kind of mess in my line of work?"

"But never so much that your bosses would want you to step back, or that your staff would act out to get to the bottom of a story."

Again, Barker waved off the possibility. "There hasn't even been an actual threat, but based on what I've uncovered with this story, they think the potential is there. Can you believe that? All this because of *potential*?"

Linus's expression turned sly. "Is that why you've been keeping a gentleman's distance from Ray? Because of the *potential* that this story could bring more to the table?"

Barker smiled in return. "You're one to ask me about

keeping 'gentleman's distances,' with Paula working around the villa all day and you cooped up here."

"Don't change the subject." A slice of Linus's earlier frustration was back.

Barker's expression darkened again. "If I go there with her, Line, the way I want to… I won't be able to stay away from her when we get back to Philly. Anyway, I think everybody's getting all panicked here for nothing."

"So it just comes down to you not wanting to take a chance with her?"

Barker let his shrug suffice for a yes.

"I get that." Linus considered what he'd been mulling over regarding unconditional love.

"The truth of it is my safety concerns aren't even at the top of the list for me keeping my distance." Barker joined Linus to stare out over the water.

"Care to share?" Linus caught the wince Barker hadn't been quick enough to mask. "Okay, now you've got to." He watched his friend launch the same kind of pensive stalk around the patio Linus had been in the midst of moments earlier.

"At first all I wanted was to sleep with her, and now…"

"You've had the chance to get to know her."

Barker winced again, adding a smirk. "Ought to be a law against women that beautiful having intelligence to match."

"Yeah…but it still wouldn't matter," Linus gave in to a smirk of his own. "We'd be tortured just the same."

Barker grinned, but soon sobered. "There's no reason for *you* to be tortured, is there? Me, on the other hand… Ray isn't a woman a man could let go of once he has her. A guy could fall in love with her quick, and that scares the hell out of me."

Barker shook his head suddenly and drew to his full height. "Fix this with Paula, man. Whatever it is. But if you think fixing it means keeping your distance from her, you're wrong. You love her and that's not changin'." He spread his hands. "All distance will do is toss you right back into the rage we've watched you battle—you don't deserve that. Neither does she." Barker patted Linus's shoulder as he made his way past.

"This place is definitely turning my brain to mush." Paula balled her fists when she arrived at the end of the pier to find who she suspected would be the only other passenger aboard the *Idella* for the evening cruise her best friend had raved about earlier.

Paula took a second to damn Sophia for her betrayal and then released a resigned sigh. She took the ramp leading to the main deck where Linus waited. "It's definitely time for me to quit my job. I'm starting to fall for the weakest lines," she said.

"My lines?" Linus guessed.

"Oh no, I'm referring to your partner in crime—Sophie," she tacked on to clarify.

Linus chuckled. "Don't be mad at her. I'm to blame for the plans changing at the last minute."

"What happened to you walking away?" Paula asked once she'd processed his words.

"I reconsidered—realized it wouldn't work to let it go that way."

She nodded, still processing everything. "And what way would work for you?"

"A way that doesn't include letting you go," he said, as though she should've known that.

"What about not making me compromise?"

"I don't expect you to."

They were interrupted before Linus could say more.

"Apologies, Mr. Brooks. We're about to cast off if that's alright."

"That's fine." Linus closed the distance to Paula and took her bag. "Take care of this, will you?" he asked the crew member.

"Linus—"

"It'll be alright," he promised with an easy smile. "I don't want us interrupted tonight."

"L, I talked to Professor Bormann."

His expression remained easy as he asked if there was anything new.

"Nothing except the next file of photos she's sending."

"Woman's dedicated," Linus commended.

"Yeah." Paula smiled. "She doesn't give up easy when she thinks she's got just cause."

"We're still talking about her nephew, Paula. A lot of women would let it go—give the guy a pass. She could still go that route." Linus paused, considering. "This is her nephew on her husband's side, right?"

"Yeah, why?"

Linus shrugged. "Maybe if the relation was closer..."

Her smile was a knowing one. "All women aren't the soft-hearted type, Line."

"Yeah…"

His hushed tone had her tilting her head out of curiosity. Paula didn't question him.

"Professor B said there'd be more candid shots in this next batch. Are you sure you haven't recognized him from the earlier files?" she asked. "Miranda Bormann's first email included property shots from her husband's estate as well as several headshots of Hayden Bormann." Still, nothing had sparked recognition for Linus or his partners.

"I'm not lying to you, P. I've never met the man." Linus's voice still held its hushed chord.

"But your staff's still digging."

He frowned then. "Well, hell yes. You never know what more there could be to the story."

"No." Paula's smile seemed sad. "No you don't. So what's the plan for tonight?" she asked, before the conversation had lingered too long in dismay. "I haven't packed anything, so if you're thinking of sailing to Havana I may need some stuff."

"You'd do that? Come away with me that far—just like that?"

She gave a flimsy shrug. "Depends on what I'd get out of it."

"I could make it worth your while."

"How?"

"Actions…words…"

"Words? Will you elaborate?"

"Later." Linus tilted his head toward the bow of the vessel. "I think the sun deserves our attention right now."

Paula agreed and happily gave herself over to the view. Yes, the sun most certainly deserved their attention. Its beauty bordered on blinding, between the glow and heat. The words were no exaggeration and yet, she wondered if they had come to mind because of the view or the man she enjoyed it with.

Slowly, Paula moved over to the bow rail. Linus joined her there soon after. They stood that way for a while before he shifted to stand behind her and secured her between himself and the railing. His hands folded on either side of her along the gleaming chrome bar of the rail.

"Linus." His name was a soft warning on her lips. "We aren't alone."

"We're about to be." His words were a murmur as his mouth traveled the slope of her neck. His lips were coaxing and soft as gossamer.

Paula tried to turn, questions on her mind. Linus wouldn't let her. "What's that supposed to mean?"

"Don't worry, the crew won't be too far away."

"Too far? Anyplace not in this boat is too far, Line."

Her anxiety had him chuckling, but his mouth never eased its journey along her nape and shoulders.

"L—"

"Hush."

Skillful fingers worked their way into the folds of her wrap. Shimmery emerald, midnight blue and hunter green material draped her curvy frame. Prepared for an evening aboard a yacht with a group of women, Paula hadn't selected sexy attire. What was the point when the night was about lazing away with girlfriends? She was regretting not being more selective then—almost.

His fingers were addictive. She could honestly never get enough of his touch. Especially when it visited its current location. With great effort, she managed to battle past arousal to recall her concerns.

"Where—" she gasped when the pad of his middle finger applied a maddening stroke to the middle of her panties "—where's the crew going?"

"They're already gone." Linus put a staying hand to her hip when he felt her jerk in response.

Paula stilled when she realized the vessel was no longer at the dock, but almost in the center of the bay. She noticed a small speedboat heading ashore.

"Wh—"

"That's for later," Linus said once he'd shushed her.

"What's for now?" she managed.

"Depends on you," he said. "The crew won't be back 'til I call them, when we're ready for dinner."

"And when's that?"

"When we're done here. We at least have to finish watching the sunset."

"I, um..." Paula had the feeling that if she remained much longer with Linus on the deck, she wouldn't be interested in the sunset. "I'm fine with watching it from wherever we're going to have dinner."

"The plan is to eat outdoors, but I'm not sure you're dressed for it."

"Sorry."

"Don't be an idiot." He smirked. "Everything's set, and I think we'll be fine outside."

"Where you've got some elaborating to do."

"Words and actions—I haven't forgotten, Paula."

"How much longer will you make me wait?"

Linus inclined his head toward the horizon. "Sun's still doin' its thing."

Once more, Paula was drawn to the sky in its myriad shades of blue and purple. "I like the way you go all out when it comes to your elaborating."

"I hope you know that's not all I have in mind." He crowded her against the railing, his mouth descending onto her nape. Both hands disappeared beneath the wrap knotted at her hip.

Massaging her waistline, Linus kissed his way across Paula's shoulders and down her back. His tongue dragged her spine. Paula fought to keep her lashes apart, but even in the face of the exquisite sunset, that proved to be an impossible feat. His kisses returned to her nape, his fingers massaging apart the wrap material until her bikini bottom was again the only barrier separating him from his prize.

"Linus—"

"Shh…it's not time for words yet."

Paula was fine with that, as words failed her miserably then. Her head fell back to his shoulder when both his middle fingers found their way inside her body. Lashes fluttering anew, she tried to keep her eyes open against the onslaught of heavy sensation.

Paula felt mesmerized, drugged even. The pleasure was that rich. Enhanced by the bewitching sunset, the pleasure struck her even more potently. Her climax hit within moments of his fingers teasing her folds to lay claim to the part of her that was already wetting his skin. The skies were darkening as she shattered for him. She became a quaking mass that hungered for more of the arousal only he could summon.

Chapter 11

To Paula's disappointment, Linus put the arousal only he could summon on hold. Her shattering climax barely scratched the surface of what she craved from him.

It would have to wait though. Paula hoped it was only a matter of waiting, and that the passing moment wasn't completely lost to them. It could be, she knew. Especially once he told her what he needed to elaborate on. She prayed it wasn't more nonsense about him letting her go for her sake.

He'd said he'd reconsidered that, which only left her mind scrambling to latch on to new reasons. Linus didn't want to let her go though and that made her happy, despite the voice that said it wasn't quite time to toss caution to the wind.

Following the all-too-brief moment of erotic bliss

on deck, he'd directed her to a nearby powder room. He'd told her the crew would be on their way back shortly, leaving Paula to wonder why they'd left in the first place. Then she'd realized their "brief" interlude on deck had lasted over a half hour. Still, to have the crew leave the vessel...had Linus been trying to protect her modesty? Did he have more fun planned for them? Paula squeezed her eyes shut, ordering her thoughts to give it a rest. She knew the man well enough to know he was a master at keeping her off kilter. He'd always been full of surprises, which had been one of the things she'd loved about him.

Paula had mourned her loss of such surprises—those off-kilter moments in her life. In a profession that required the ability to anticipate every surprise, it would've been nice to enjoy a private life where shake-ups of the delightful variety were possible.

Was she on the verge of recapturing that lost element? She hoped so. Now that she had Linus back in her life, she didn't want to lose him. Dammit! That was the *one* place she hadn't wanted to find herself when this all started. She wouldn't deny the truth though. She didn't want to lose him a second time.

Paula took a moment to summon calm to soothe her ragged thoughts. The powder room, like the rest of the yacht, was a relaxing space. The wide oval mirror flattered the reflection even as it provided soft lighting from the small bulbs encircling it. The plush white rug beneath her feet was a beautiful contrast against the chestnut brown walls and gold fixtures. She curled her toes into its thickness and took solace in the small luxury.

She wouldn't lose him a second time, she vowed. Even if it did mean compromising herself to do it. This wasn't about avoiding uncomfortable truths—not completely. The simple fact was that the man she still loved had real horrors from his past. And they affected his present. She had witnessed those effects firsthand during the brief time they'd been back in each other's lives.

Paula had come to the conclusion that she didn't care to have him revisit such a past. She could do without the explanations or elaborations she felt she was owed if it meant sparing him a return to something that unsettled him that way.

What she wanted was time—time they'd been brutally robbed of. If explanations of the past surfaced in the midst of it, well, she'd take what she could get.

Paula discovered the crew had other reasons for leaving the yacht beyond giving her and Linus their privacy. The small speedboat she'd witnessed heading for shore had been transporting the crew to the spot where they were getting things prepared for a candlelit dinner along the shore.

The dinner, however, was only part of what had Paula speechless when Linus escorted her from the *Idella*. A large tent had been erected some twenty feet behind the intimately set table for two. Despite the aromas that had her stomach churning from hunger, she was more interested in finding out what was behind the closed beige and black construction.

Linus smoothly directed her path, keeping her on course toward the dinner table.

"What are you up to, L?" Paula queried slyly as though she didn't really expect him to tell her.

"Elaboration," was all he'd say, and waved toward the table.

They sat and were served by the dutiful crew. To drink, it was a fragrant wine for Paula, one of Linus's preferred foreign brews for him. They drank in silence for a while. Once again, their eyes were both fixed on the sky that was aglow with hordes of stars.

Paula reveled in the sight, tossing her head back toward the night breezes her gaze took a lazy scan of the heavens. When she risked a glance to see if Linus was as riveted as she was, his eyes were on her face.

The crew began to serve while he started his story.

"She could've left us to be raised by anyone in the family," he said of his grandmother who took in him and his brother following the deaths of their parents in a chartered plane crash.

"Anyone would've taken us," Linus continued, his fierce features appearing more intense in the wake of the memory. "They all knew how much we mattered to her—knew her money would one day be our money—but she wanted to be the one to raise us." He studied the night view and shook his head. "Some in the family said it was because she wanted to make up for the time she and my granddad spent building the family business."

Paula nodded, recalling that the Brooks owned a chain of textile factories across the northeast. Today, only a few members of the family were needed on hand for day-to-day management, as the businesses were so well envisioned they practically ran themselves.

"Guess all the hard work was worth it. Those two single-handedly turned my grandfather's entire family into members of the elite class." His smile turned sardonic, the mood further sharpening his features.

"Whatever the reason, she raised us better than anyone else could have," he went on. "Whoever said the privileged were coldhearted never met her. Her heart was bigger than she was. In the end it was her downfall."

He shifted in his chair then, as though he were considering standing. Yet he remained seated. "When she loved, it was unconditionally, whether the target of her love deserved it or not."

"Your brother," Paula guessed.

"My grandmother wasn't your average wealthy widow," Linus resumed once they'd been served.

There was a light garden salad set to the side of a small bowl of shrimp étouffée. The main course was a grilled fillet of salmon on a bed of mixed vegetables.

"She lived very modestly—well below her means. She wasn't doing it to teach the value of frugality. It's just who she was." The softness that had crept into his rich gaze hardened. "My brother wasn't like that. According to him, what was the point of frugal living if you had the money to cover the bill?"

Paula helped herself to the étouffée. "Guess your brother and grandmother had some heated talks over *that* difference of opinion."

"Yeah." Linus cut into his salmon. "The differences

turned into some major battles. It got ugly, but she never stopped trying to change his mind—or his habits. She was a smart woman but…blind to so much. She thought it was all a stage, something he'd outgrow. He never did."

"What didn't he outgrow?"

"Gambling. His messes got bigger and she kept digging him out—kept digging until she gave out."

Paula set down took her fork, which had been poised for a corner of the tender salmon, and reached for Linus's hand. "I'm sorry, L."

He placed a hard kiss to the back of her hand. "I think she would've kept it up—kept bailing him out until she had nothing left to give." Linus studied her hand as he spoke.

Paula lifted her hand and smoothed her thumb across his cheek. "She left everything to *you,* remember? I think she would've left him to clean his own mess eventually."

"But why'd she have to die to do it, Paula?" With a relieved sigh, he returned to eating. "The night I…lost it with you, my brother came to warn me that you might take my money one day. The very next minute, he was asking for another bailout. Him coming there and tracking me down to encourage me to question your motives, while trying to run his same game on me…for a while I considered letting him. I tried to make myself see past his selfish entitled surface the way my gran did, but I…"

Linus shook his head and attacked his food with more gusto. "I didn't rip his head off though. I held my temper…'til I got back, anyway, and then…" He wolfed down more food.

Paula ate as well, and the moment passed in easy silence for well over two minutes.

"I guess that's why I'm so determined to help Miranda Bormann," she said finally. "Without her, I wouldn't have been able to accomplish half of what I have. Forget about being anyone's DA."

"I disagree," Linus chimed in after swigging down his preferred beer. "I wasn't surprised a bit when you got the seat. I always knew your confidence would take you places. I prayed what happened to us wouldn't touch that."

"Thanks, L, but I've got Professor B to credit for a lot of my confidence." She forked off another flaky morsel of the rapidly disappearing salmon and spoke around it.

"Miranda Bormann was my law school professor, but I really got to know her during undergrad. I'd gotten work study in the law library and was there one day when she came in, harried and on her way to give a talk she hadn't prepared for. The library kept copies of all her talks, and she was sure there'd be something in the archives she could use. She said it'd have to be something dated so the audience wouldn't easily recall it was a repeat." Paula smiled over the memory.

"Anyway, after she gave me a rundown of the event and topic, I did a little creative searching and found something that worked. She was impressed and started tapping me to assist with locating materials for her classes. Then one day, she offered me a job. Work study was a requirement of my financial aid, so the arrangement stood."

Across the table, Linus smiled. He enjoyed the soft light that had crept into her eyes as she recalled happier days.

"The only 'work' I did was to get her coffee and our lunches, which were…spectacular. The woman knows her food. Hmph." Paula's smile grew wider. "She told me the thing was called work study, and she wanted me studying."

"So you got paid to study. Nice. Every student should be so lucky." Linus drew another long gulp from his brew.

"That was Professor B," Paula said, toying with a flyaway curl from her upswept hair as she spoke. "By the time I was a student in her class, I'd already learned more than I ever could have from *any* book. It's hard to unlearn a lifetime of being thought of as less. That kind of treatment takes a toll."

Paula's expression was a pensive one as she studied the sublime night sky. "It makes you doubt yourself and accept the doubt because you've been told for years you're worth nothing more. I was just an inner city girl from a broken home. My mom could claim one of at least twenty men as my father."

She left the table then, refusing to let the ideas take hold and direct her moods as they so easily could. "Professor B wouldn't let me use any of that as an excuse—wouldn't let me cower from what needed to be done and use self-doubt as the reason."

Linus left the table then too. He couldn't stand the

lonely figure she made as she looked out over the calm water. Taking her arm, he drew her back against him. Though the breeze claimed a pleasant warmth, her skin rose with gooseflesh just the same when his palms grazed her skin. Paula leaned into his mouth when it caressed her ear.

"I never thought you were less, Paula. Not even when I was acting like a prick. I never believed that."

"I know that, Linus. I know it," Paula repeated when she turned in his arms. "That's why it took a minute for me to stop trying to make you snap out of whatever had come over you that night. I—it was like you were a different person."

Linus muttered something indecipherable and set his forehead against hers. Easing back, he kissed her there before letting his mouth trail her temple. The sensation was like velvet petals against her skin, and Paula leaned into his mouth again while smiling her approval.

"I'll never be able to tell you enough how sorry I am, Paula."

"I don't really care about it right now." With that, she stood on her toes to take his tempting mouth with hers. Gently, she outlined the shape of his lips. Soon after, she felt her feet leaving the sand.

Linus had allowed her to pull on only a wrap she'd kept from her bag before he'd whisked her into a speedboat that carried them to the remote shore. The night had been pleasantly warm, but its slightly cooler temperature now continued to rouse the gooseflesh along her bare skin.

Linus dragged her up against him, and her entire

body flooded with microscopic chills. Instinctively, Paula curved her legs about his waist, her arms doing the same at his neck. Their kiss was scorchingly infectious, to the point where they were both moaning their appreciation by the time Linus began their trip to the tent.

The doting crew had made themselves scarce by then. Paula scanned the area through half-lidded, arousal-drugged eyes. She managed to observe, while Linus devoured her neck, that the tent flaps had been drawn open. Soft, golden illumination poured from the interior, and she was curious to know what lay beyond.

Alas, her curiosity had no chance of holding out against Linus's prowess. Paula just managed to catch a glimpse of the interior that ran to a soothing color scheme of wood browns and beige; gold accents outlined the massive bed. Aside from an oversized linen-draped chair and end tables, the bed was the only furnishing.

It was all they needed. Their frenzied kissing had resumed. Linus's open shirt had tantalized Paula with an unobstructed view of his sinfully sculpted chest. She made fast work of shoving it to the ground. Losing interest in her surroundings, she was completely focused on Linus at work on her body.

His tongue courted hers with a tormenting fervor—possessive, sultry, ruthless. Paula could barely summon the ability to engage. She was far more fixed on letting her mouth be taken by his skillful thrusts. The rotations swirled about her tongue before his lips suckled it. The strokes caressed her teeth and the roof and sides of her mouth before he withdrew, only to repeat the process.

It was Paula withdrawing next, breaking away in an effort to communicate to him that she needed a moment. Linus wasn't in the mood to oblige and launched his next assault on her ear. His activities there were just as overwhelming and ruthless. She barely felt them moving as he closed the space to the stunning bed and she shivered the moment her bare skin contacted the suede, maple-brown comforter.

Linus stopped Paula from making the effort to tug herself from her bikini. Smoothly, he claimed her wrists, anchoring them above her head while his teeth snagged one of the frail ties that secured her top, ruining it. One tug and the garment loosened at her chest.

"Dammit, L—"

"Shh." He nudged aside the material. "Just wear the wrap when we leave."

"The crew will know what we've been doing," she hissed.

"Do you think they wouldn't know anyway?" He chuckled.

Paula wanted to laugh too, but she gasped instead. Linus's gifted tongue had encircled a pouting nipple, licking it until it glistened before he treated it to an achingly sweet suckle. Her body bowed beneath his. She braced at his hold on her wrists, only to feel it grow firm. She was where he wanted her, and it was where he intended to keep her—for the time being at least.

His quiet moans brought Paula almost as much pleasure as what he was doing to her breasts. She couldn't imagine that such devouring was as enjoyable as actually *being* devoured, but Linus seemed as powerfully satisfied as she was, if the sounds vibrating from his throat were any example.

The next sound Paula uttered was a sob. Linus abandoned her well-tended breasts. His tongue swept their undersides before trailing her rib cage and navel. He released her wrists, but she was too drunk with passion to move them straightaway. Her fingers curved into the comforter as his curved around the ties of her bikini bottom. She winced in expectation of hearing the fabric rip, but Linus surprised her by dutifully pulling the strings to relieve her of the material. Paula clutched at the tangled comforter then. The tip of Linus's nose charted a leisurely course across her waxed mound before his tongue feathered across her clit, seconds prior to his lips treating it to a light suckle.

Linus cradled her hips lightly, and then he was trading the embrace for a more secure one about her thighs. He took her with his tongue, and her body bowed once again. Linus withdrew momentarily to nibble at the powder-soft folds of her sex and soothe the spot beneath his nose. Then the series of thrusts and nibbles resumed.

The sequence continued, driving Paula more and more insane with need. When he stopped altogether, he took her mouth before she could utter one word in protest. His shirt was already a distant memory, and she sought to sentence his pants to the same fate.

Instead of stopping her, Linus assisted, shoving down the material as he kicked out of the leather sandals he'd worn with lightweight sweats. He reached up to knock aside a few of the pillows bunched along the head of the bed and retrieved a stash of condoms.

"Planning to keep me up all night?" she asked.

"All night—and then all morning," he clarified.

It sounded like heaven to Paula. Her heart pounded fiercely as she watched him tear into one of the foil packets. Paula used the momentary distraction to her advantage. Shoving Linus to his back, she took the open packet and proceeded to apply their protection.

Linus was poised to put Paula on her back again and tried to press the issue when she resisted. He was mad to have her, but relented when she begged in the nicest way as she settled over him, sheathing his sex inside hers.

"I like the way you beg," he said.

"Don't get used to it," she purred.

"I'm pretty sure I have a few things I could make you beg for."

"You're putting your life in serious jeopardy if you try." Her last few words were a gasp as she succumbed to sensations that spider-webbed beneath her skin until she was trembling with desire and the preliminary rumbles of orgasm.

Her body turned to syrup, and she would've been wilting over Linus had he not taken charge. Cupping her waist, his hold was secure even as it guided her up and down his wide, dark length. Linus squeezed his eyes shut as the rumbles of his own orgasm began to take shape. Paula's body was plump and ripe for his taking. She was everything he wanted and always had been. Still, it was her strength, boldness and intelligence that truly beckoned. Those were the elements that lasted.

"I love you," he said.

"I know you do."

She laughed as she said the words, and Linus realized she thought he was teasing or basing his emotion on the pleasure she brought him. He gave himself over to her quickly then, groaning deeply when he erupted inside the condom. Paula responded with a shuddering gasp and desperately squeezed his throbbing erection to absorb the vibrations of his release. She'd been in the grips of her own climax when Linus entered his. Now, those sensations were overpowering her at an intense, impossible rate. She was still shuddering when he put her on her back.

"I love you."

He repeated the phrase in a way that cut through the haze of erotic bliss. Paula understood then. He hadn't meant the words as a lighthearted reference to their sexual activity. She was sorry she'd indicated that he had.

"I love you, Linus. I—"

He didn't give her the chance for more words, which were going to be ones of apology over misunderstanding him. He was kissing her again, deeply, searchingly, absorbingly.

Paula moaned twice in rapid succession when she felt his shaft transform from its state of semi-hardness to its rigid, thrusting power. He cursed with vicious suddenness and withdrew. Quickly, he applied a fresh condom and returned to glove himself to the hilt inside her. The act replayed itself many times over that night and into the morning.

Linus woke with a sigh. He'd recalled the rain ushering them into sleep as they dozed off well after dawn that morning. He wasn't sure how long they'd slept or if they'd slept the day away. The light streaming into the tent was strangely dim. Then he heard the distinctive patter against the outer fabric. More rain. The realization had his eyelids drooping closed again in preparation for another long snooze.

Paula was still unconscious next to him. She slept on her stomach, her lovely face half-hidden in a pillow. She looked both sated and depleted. Linus's dimpled smile firmed. He was quite proud of the role he had played in making that happen. The rain patter intensified slightly, and he was moving to cage Paula beneath him, his plan to rejoin her in sleep, when he heard another distinctive sound.

The crew had been instructed—warned, really—not to disturb them once they were inside the tent. As his friends were busy with their own interests, Linus was sure it wasn't them. Given that, all else was secondary. His vibrating phone silenced, only to resume seconds later. Why hadn't he thought to put the damn thing on silent? It hadn't been much of a bother, that's why. Paula's had been the aggravation, which was why he'd insisted on her leaving her bag behind when they'd left the boat.

With a sigh, he grabbed his sweats from the wide rug on his side of the enormous bed. The vibrating had stopped again and had not resumed. Linus checked the screen and felt his heart lurch when he saw who had called. He'd asked Estella not to bother contacting him unless she'd found something. Evidently she had.

The phone buzzed, that time to indicate a voice message. Linus glanced back to see that Paula was still sleeping and activated the message. As he listened, his relaxed state of the past several hours mutated into one that had him brushing a lingering kiss on Paula's back and then leaving the bed to get dressed.

Chapter 12

Linus had the speedboat cart him back to the villa. He celebrated the fact that he wouldn't have to interrupt his partners from more enjoyable activities when he found Eli and Tig in the main sitting area. The long, low coffee table there was covered in laser-printed photos and other documents. Tig was the first to notice Linus entering.

"Ah! Just the man we wanted to see," Tig called.

Linus caught the slightly less than playful chord in Tig's words. He flicked a curious glance toward the cluttered white-topped table.

"Just got off the phone with Este," he said instead of inquiring about the state of the table. "I had a feeling and asked her to check on something for me. It, um..." Linus made his way deeper into the room. "It was just a feeling. I didn't plan on her to find anything when I asked her to look."

Eli and Tig shared a quick look. They knew better than most that Linus's "feelings" were like gold. The man had a perception that was unmatched.

"What do you know?" Eli asked.

"I asked her to find all that she could on Miranda Bormann."

"And?" Eli probed.

Linus smirked. "Something simple, really. Right before our eyes the whole time. I just didn't think to ask. That dossier Paula drew up had everything except info on the woman herself."

"Bormann?" Tig queried. "But she gave us everything, Line. Info on the woman's work, her passions after retirement…"

"But what about the simplest information?" Linus countered, and there was a hint of amusement in his voice then. "You guys wanna guess what her middle name is?"

Eli and Tig settled back in their chairs. Realization was already alight on their handsome faces. Tig was first to make a move. Leaning forward, he reached for one of the photographs and extended it to Linus.

"Guess this won't really surprise you." Tig sighed.

"A lot of the property her father-in-law owned went to her late husband," Eli explained as Linus moved in closer to take the photo.

"Being the oldest," Eli continued, "Henry Bormann inherited what wasn't already earmarked for charity."

"That's the family castle in Yorkshire, England," Tig

explained. “They own two others—one in Scotland and the other in New Zealand. That’s a family photo taken when they all visited for Christmas two years before her husband passed. The guy wearing the bandana is her nephew, Hayden Bormann. Recognize who he’s got in a headlock?”

Linus could feel his mouth tightening. “I’ll be damned,” he murmured.

Paula woke and was on the verge of purring; she felt just that blissful. She hesitated on giving in to the urge, unsure of how alone she was. The splatter of water against the tent tempted her to return to sleep, but she resisted.

Besides, Linus was gone so there’d be no tempting from that end. He had left her a parting message though. That was enough to keep the relaxing vibes flowing. He had needed to see his partners and hadn’t wanted to wake her. The crew would be on hand to carry her back to the villa when she was ready. Her bag was on the chair near the bed, but she was in no hurry to dive into it. She was more interested in reminiscing over the previous evening.

She couldn’t have planned it more perfectly. The “I love yous” they had exchanged had been the cherries on top, and they were more than enough.

The statement replayed in her head with a finality that left no doubts in her mind. Not only was Linus Brooks the man she loved, he was the man she would no longer allow the past to keep her away from.

The sound of the popping bottle cap turned Paula’s

focus to her bag. She scooted up and over to snag the tote from the chair. She was pretty much awake anyway, and guessed she may as well use the time to get a little work done. Sure, it was work, but in such exquisite surroundings, who could complain?

Paula dug the phone from the deep recesses of the bag and read the notification of a new email. Miranda Bormann. Paula made a mental note to call the woman later. If she didn't get around to calling then, chances were very high that they wouldn't talk for another couple of days.

Rook and Viva's wedding was scheduled for the following day. It was sure to be a lively period between that night and the next. Paula was sure she wouldn't be in any mood to discuss business of any sort for at least another twenty-four hours beyond that.

Activating her email with one hand, she used the other to squish pillows behind her back. The handy paper clip icon alongside the notification told her there was a file attached. Paula gave Miranda Bormann's message a cursory scan and smiled at her promise that this was the LAST ONE and that she was going to leave her alone to enjoy the rest of her trip.

Paula saw that the file she opened consisted of five images. She was about to hit forward to send it on to Linus, Eli and Tig when she gave the fourth photo another look.

And realized that enjoying the rest of her trip now would be impossible.

She was on the beach when he found her, seated in the sand along the stretch that ran past her suite. Linus thought back to the solitary figure she'd made the night before when she had talked of being used to thought of as less—as a nonentity. He wondered then if she was thinking the same in that moment or worse—that she had been played for a fool.

He could tell when she'd sensed his presence, and he ceased his advance toward her.

"You know," was all he said.

"Know what?" Paula continued to hug her knees, curling her toes into the gleaming sand. It was cool, given the earlier rain and overcast skies that had remained throughout the day. The wind was brisk, and she welcomed its stirring strength as it hit her face and ruffled her hair.

"Do I know that this is the place Miranda Bormann's nephew is trying to sell out from under her? Yeah. Yeah, I know."

Her voice was level and carried no hint of a temper. The fact unsettled Linus all the more. He had snuck away from the office enough times to watch her in court. He'd observed her on many occasions using that cool tone before she dropped the anvil that eviscerated some guilty soul and paved the way for conviction.

"Would you believe I only found out this morning?" Linus adopted the easy tone that never failed to benefit him when it came to business.

Paula's light eyes remained on the active waves. "Does it matter?"

Linus closed what distance remained between them and dropped to the sand next to her. "You're damn right it matters when you're sitting here trying to decide if you can trust me again. I just found out this morning, Paula."

"Linus—"

"I asked Estella to run a deep background check on Miranda Bormann." He returned the stony look she gave him with a level expression. "I wanted to know more about Miranda Bormann before she became Mrs. Henry Randolph Bormann. When she was Miranda Hartman. Miranda Claudette Hartman. Claudette's Key? Her husband named the place—*this* place—after her. It was too much of a coincidence for it not to be true.

"It was why I left you this morning. Este called to give me the report. I only asked her to look for one thing—whether Miranda Bormann had a connection to *this* place." Linus cast a weary look around their oasis and shook his head. "This was the one place—the one thing we hadn't thought to question. I came back here to talk it over with Eli and Tig, and they showed me this." He took a printed photo image from a pocket of his canvas shorts.

"That's the Bormann family at their castle in England," he said when Paula took the page. "Hayden Bormann is wearing the bandana. He's got his cousin, Calvin Maxton, in a headlock."

"Maxton." Paula repeated the name.

"Our connection for the job we've been sitting in the middle of for over a week. He's the one I met with, Paula. I'm not sure why Hayden Bormann was at Joss the day Miranda Bormann's detective tailed him there, but it is what it is."

Paula's smile was a study in resignation. "Just like that."

Linus nodded, as though he'd been waiting for her to challenge the explanation. "Say what you need to, P."

"I thought I just did."

"I must've missed it."

"Alright." Paula studied the sand around her feet. "Missing things? *You?* The man who has half the folks in Philly quaking in their high-powered boots over the mere mention of having to meet with you? Something they'd do anyway, since they can barely resist salivating over the idea of having Joss lead one of their projects."

"It happens." Linus's expression was unreadable. "Or are you saying I can't make mistakes? I think you know better… I missed this, Paula. It couldn't have been plainer than the nose on my face, and I missed it. That's no lie. I didn't lie to you about any of it."

"Oh, L, I know that." She didn't hesitate over the admission. She didn't want to.

Still, Linus didn't give the impression that he was reassured. "And yet there you sit, debating over whether that makes you a fool."

Paula shook her head, and Linus wondered if she'd sensed the defiant edge to the gesture. Was she trying to convince herself, or only looking the part?

"I'll, um, I'm gonna get out of here, Paula."

"Linus, wait—"

"It's alright, babe."

"I thought we were past all this, L. Like maybe after last night we turned a corner—like we were getting another chance." She scooted to her knees in the sand. "I know it could mean compromise—" She hesitated, spotting him bristle.

"I know you have trouble with that, L, but isn't that what the best relationships are about? Compromise?"

Linus leaned in to brush several windblown curls from her face. "They're also about communication," he said. "I haven't done much of that though, have I?"

She squeezed his hand, kissed the back of it. "I got up this morning ready to see what today and the next would bring and then…" She sighed, lifted her hands toward the gray skies. "Then all this…it's quite a turnaround, wouldn't you say?"

Linus studied the active waves as he nodded. "I guess you're right."

"Maybe we both just need time to wrap our heads around it."

Linus continued to toy with Paula's hair. "That's what I'm trying to give you now." It was what he was trying to give them both. Time to wrap his head around the fact that this trip might end with them in a worse spot than they'd been at the outset. He couldn't tolerate the idea of walking away from her, and yet…that might be all there was left to do. He struck the possibility from his mind and forced a smile. "Stay put." He bumped her chin with his fist. "Enjoy the quiet while you can. This place is gonna be a madhouse by this time tomorrow." He put a hasty kiss to her forehead and then let another—that one a little more leisurely—slide down her temple.

The peck to her cheek was repeated against her mouth before his tongue teased her lips apart to taste her with gentle strokes. Paula moaned, ready for more.

When she tugged at his shirt though, he took her hands, squeezing them, and set her away from his clothes.

He put a kiss to her ear then. “I love you,” he said, and was gone.

Chapter 13

Linus's prediction—that the island would be a madhouse by the following afternoon—was terribly accurate. The madhouse feel was evident early the following morning, though there was no overabundance of furnishings, and no floral arrangements were needed. As the nuptials were to take place in such an idyllic setting, natural beauty did the majority of the work.

Sophia, as the great orchestrator of her big sister's perfect day, had arranged for a sunrise event. Planners had arrived at sunrise the morning prior to begin setting the stage. And they weren't the only ones working at such an early hour.

The *Idella*'s crew had been en route hours earlier. The *Idella* was headed to Nassau to collect the first of the eighty-some odd guests set to attend. While the groom's guest list was a relatively modest one, the bride's was a little more extensive. Those connected to the Hail family had insisted on being there, given they'd felt cheated out of joining in on Sophia's nuptials.

Additionally, there were those connected to Viva's Hollywood career who insisted on attending as well. Sophia gave herself several pats on the back for keeping the guest list to such a manageable number.

Paula made her way up to the dining room shortly after the yacht departed to collect the first of the guests. A midnight breakfast was presented buffet style, which pleased her greatly. She wasn't in the mood for small talk. Besides, there would be more than enough time for that later.

She filled a plate with eggs, medallion biscuits, sausage, fruit and cheese. Coffee in hand, she ventured out to study the beach instead of heading back to her suite straightaway. Another wedding, she mused, sipping the rich Colombian brew and silently reveling as it flooded her bloodstream. Had anything truly changed since the last one she'd attended? Had anything improved? Things had changed, she acknowledged, while setting her plate to the small stone table perched by the walls that overlooked the shore.

It appeared the girl she'd been and the woman she'd become had joined forces. The woman had been conspicuously silent since the onset of the trip. Paula hadn't complained. She didn't regret anything that had happened between her and Linus, regardless of the Miranda Bormann revelations. Still, she'd expected more tension to rise afterward. Perhaps there was nothing else left to stand between them...but what of the rest of his story? It still haunted him, and she ached to share that load with him.

The aroma of breakfast called to her then, and she set away her questions in hopes that a full stomach might help her make more sense of her thoughts.

It sounded like a pretty good plan. Too bad she wasn't buying it.

The Hail sisters were at last on equal footing as far as the planning of spectacular weddings. The sunrise event was a sight rivaled only by that made by Rook and Viva.

Beautiful and in love, the two spoke vows entwined with devotion and desire. Once the couple was pronounced man and wife, Rook took Viva in his arms and told their guests that they had only a short while to mingle. The newlyweds planned to set out on their honeymoon by midmorning.

The island had become a loud and lively destination. Laughter and conversation consumed almost every square inch of the villa. Paula enjoyed herself more than she'd expected. She hadn't seen Linus during the wedding or the reception, but didn't make a real effort to seek him out until everyone gathered at the dock to wave off Rook and Viva. The *Idella* was set to carry them back to Nassau, where they'd board a private jet to the Maldives.

Paula had returned to the villa before the boat cleared the bay. She checked Linus's suite, but there was no trace of him there. It was a while before she saw anyone she'd arrived with and had all but given up the search when she noticed Tig working his way through the crowd. She went to meet him.

"Tigo!" With a wave, Paula jostled her way closer to the man. "Where's Linus?"

Apology immediately filled Tig's dark eyes. "Sorry, hon. He, uh, he left last night when the *Idella* started making its first trips to Nassau for the guests."

"Why?" Paula shook her head in confusion.

"What came out about Miranda Bormann hit him pretty hard." Tig squeezed Paula's forearm in a calming gesture. "Not only because of what's going on with the two of you—"

"Oh, Tig, there's nothing—"

Tig interrupted with a sly smile. "You think women are the only ones who talk about relationships and regrets? Linus brought you here to fix whatever happened between you, to apologize for it *and* to tell you why it happened."

"Do *you* know why it happened?" Paula asked, her tone uneasy and hesitant.

"I know what you're asking, Paula, and no, no I don't. I don't think anybody's ever known because I don't think he's ever really shared it with anybody."

"Yeah." Paula's uncertainty meshed with sadness.

Tig squeezed her forearm again. "He loves you."

"I know, Tig. I knew it when everything was falling apart." She gave an attempt at providing a refreshing sigh. "So where'd he go?"

"Back to Philly. He wanted to get things ready for the meeting with Calvin Maxton."

"Meeting?"

"The plan is to let Maxton know our trip here was a success and that we want to share our brainstorming ideas with everyone on his end who'd have to sign off on it."

Discovery filled Paula's eyes. "You're hoping he'll bring Hayden Bormann."

Tig inclined his head, which was confirmation enough for Paula. "We'll make sure Maxton knows that if we meet any newcomers after this meeting, we'll take it as a sign of dishonesty, and the deal will be null and Linus will be extremely pissed." He smirked. "There aren't many who don't know what happens when Linus is pissed."

Paula nodded, able to imagine that all too well.

"It's been years since we've seen him lose his temper—really lose it." Tig's voice carried a mildly haunted quality. "I'd hate for him to break the streak he fought so hard to get and hold on to, but this…" He raked a hand through his hair and muttered a curse. "He's taking this all very personally—the fact that he missed Maxton being foul." Tig took two flutes of champagne from a passing waiter and offered one to Paula.

"The blame for missing anything probably rests on my shoulders," she said.

"Paula—"

"He was distracted—that's because of me." She sipped her drink. "I was distracted by him. If I wasn't, I might've thought to ask Professor B to send photos of all her husband's family properties first. It makes sense that her nephew would choose a personal holding to lay the foundation for a shady business deal."

"Paula." Tig took her glass and set it, along with his, atop the ledge they stood closest to. He took her shoulders and gave her a gentle squeeze. "You don't need to do this. Right now you need to finish this thing with Hayden Bormann so you two can get on with your lives together. Think on that and nothing else. Alright?" He watched her a moment longer and then squeezed her arms again before moving on.

Paula let her eyes drift toward the bay. The beauty of Claudette's Key remained unchanged, but Paula felt herself longing for snowcapped skyscrapers and chilly winds. She was ready to go home.

Chapter 14

Philadelphia, Pennsylvania
Four Days Later

Paula admitted she may've been thinking a smidge rashly when she'd longed for the chilly winds and snow-capped 'scrapers of home. She'd returned from sun and fragrant flora to find her town a virtual ice cube. The 'scrapers weren't quite snowcapped, yet the consistent frost of the overnight hours had left them with a thin dusting of white. It held not only to the rooftops, but railings and curbs as well.

Messy as it may've been to some, for Paula it infused her with an understated courage. It was something she believed she'd need during the meeting she was on her way to. She hadn't seen or spoken to Linus since their afternoon together on the beach. He'd made no effort to reach out to her, even after she'd called to RSVP to his invite for the Maxton meeting. She'd spoken only with his assistant, who'd said her presence was encouraged.

Paula and Miranda Bormann arrived at the Joss offices that afternoon just past 1:00 p.m.

"Oh my, is that him?"

Paula frowned over Miranda Bormann's breathy comment and then followed the woman's fixed stare across the room. They had been shown to one of the corner conference areas. The meeting would begin in less than a half hour.

Paula cleared her throat quietly when she saw Linus speaking with Bormann's investigator, Rick Lurie, and his associates.

"Yeah." She forced out the word in a hushed tone when she felt Bormann's eyes on her.

"Goodness, girl, how'd you stand walking away from a thing of beauty like that?"

"I wasn't the one who walked away."

"Oh, honey." Bormann pulled Paula aside. "I'm so sorry."

"It's nothing, Professor B—"

"Shh now." Miranda Bormann gave an impatient shake of her head. "I can imagine how that had to sting, and to go through it twice in a lifetime…" Again, she shook her head. "I couldn't imagine having to say goodbye to my Henry that way."

Paula gave the woman's shoulders a slight shake. "You don't have anything to apologize for—I wanted to help. I owe you for what I've become."

"No, Paula, you owe that to working your ass off, and you owe it to yourself to be happy. Don't let this stop that."

"I'm not." Paula looked toward Linus again. "I'm not, but I think *he* is. We were right there, and then all this. I think it has him believing he's disappointed me or something—thinking we're back to where we were the night everything went crazy."

"Have you told him that's not true?"

Paula smiled sadly, then shook her head. "I haven't really had the chance. Hmph…maybe I just haven't taken the chance."

"Tsk, tsk…" The retired professor shook her head, but playfulness brightened her eyes. "My love, haven't you learned a thing from what I've taught you? Sometimes the chance—in all its perfect timing—never comes. You just have to make your move and pray for the best." Before Paula could respond, Bormann was pushing past her to extend a hand to Linus and looking up at him with a savory smile.

Linus accepted the handshake. "Glad to meet you, Dr. Bormann. I wish it wasn't under these circumstances."

Miranda Bormann gave a playful sigh. "If it weren't for these circumstances, chances are we wouldn't be meeting at all, unless—" she regarded Paula with a quick, sly look "—you're going to make an honest woman out of my favorite student."

"I'm working on it, Professor." Linus looked to Paula as well and then back to Bormann. "Your nephews should be here soon."

Bormann appeared to shudder. "Ingrates. They've made me happy I never became a mother."

"I'm sorry, Dr. Bormann."

Bormann waved away Linus's apology. "I'm the one who should be apologizing for interfering with what was surely a very satisfying trip."

"Professor B…"

Linus grinned over Paula's admonishing tone. "Protecting my business is very important to me, Dr. Bormann. Thank you for going to Paula and encouraging her to come to me."

Bormann patted Linus's forearm. "I'll leave you two to talk."

Linus's smile remained while his eyes followed Bormann's departure. "She's somethin' else."

"You don't know the half." Paula smiled as well and then looked to Linus. "Back on the island, I was surprised to hear you'd left."

"I needed to get back and fix this."

Paula studied the muscle dancing along his strong jaw. "What exactly is 'this'?" She swallowed at the steadiness of his eyes trained on hers.

"This is me doing my job, Paula." His gaze continued its trek across her mouth, neck and chest.

Paula forbid herself to swoon beneath its potency and latched on to the next conversation piece that entered her mind. "My holiday party—I, um, I invited you. Will you be there?"

"I want to be—"

"Sorry for the interruption, Linus, DA Starker." Joss

assistant Desmond Wallace gave Paula an apologetic smile before whispering something to Linus.

Linus sent Desmond away with a nod before turning back to Paula. He squeezed her hand and left her.

Calvin Maxton was all big grins and sparkling eyes when he was shown into Eli's office.

"Santigo! Linus! Eli!" Maxton greeted the partners with hearty handshakes before turning to the man who had accompanied him.

"My partner, Hayden Bormann." Maxton offered an uncertain smile when it appeared that the Joss partners weren't interested in additional handshakes.

"You say Mr. Bormann is your partner?" Tig said, in an apparent effort to set the meeting on its intended course. "There's gotta be more than that—you guys look like brothers."

"But not as close as that, right?" Eli guessed.

"No," Linus answered. "Not as close as that."

Maxton and Bormann traded looks laced with a silent message that something wasn't right.

"Have we missed something?" Maxton queried with a shaky laugh.

"No, but I did." Linus sighed, the sound not at all comforting. "Claudette's Key. Your aunt's got a nice middle name—Claudette."

Discovery surged in the cousins' gazes. Then Maxton was moving close to Linus with his hands outstretched, as though an apology was forthcoming.

"Save it," Linus said.

"I'd do what he says," Tig added. "We aren't keen

to have bloodshed on the premises, but we may turn a blind eye in this case. Linus." Tig turned the floor back over to his partner.

"Let's hear from your cousin, Cal," Linus decided, taking a slow turn around the room. "We know it was his idea to suggest this project and have you act as the front man. You're brave to show up here, Bormann. We know you're trying to stay under the radar of the detective your aunt hired."

Hayden Bormann managed a modicum of coolness. "She won't be thinking about detectives in a few weeks. She'll be too busy thinking of all the money about to flood her accounts when we start booking suites at the villa."

"The land isn't yours to do anything with," Eli reminded him. "Legally it belongs to Miranda Claudette Bormann."

"And you guys care about this why?" Hayden Bormann snapped. "Your bank accounts are already singing from the preliminary payments we've made. As per our agreement, you're entitled to a share of the profits from our inaugural bookings. Our call center is already taking reservation requests."

"You think our agreement's still valid after this?" Tig almost laughed.

"My aunt's finances haven't suffered." Hayden Bormann gave a flip of his hand. "I never shifted any funds that weren't immediately replaced."

"That's funny how you make 'shifted' sound like 'stole,'" Eli noted.

Bormann bristled. “Check her books. You’ll see I’m telling the truth.”

“For a change.”

The men turned collectively when a door opened and Miranda Bormann stepped into the conference room. Joining her was Paula, the professor’s private investigators and a few others.

Miranda Bormann approached her nephews. A moment later the room echoed with the vicious slaps she laid to their faces. “You’re nothing but stains on the family name. You’ve been millionaires since birth and that’s still not enough.”

“Aunty Mir—”

“I hope you’re not about to say you just wanted something of your own.” Miranda Bormann’s expression was a knowing one. “You always were such a hilarious child, Hayden. Did you think I’d find this funny?”

Subdued, Hayden Bormann looked toward the floor. “I put it all back.”

“And you thought that would make this alright?” the woman hissed back to her nephew.

“Aunt Miranda.” Calvin Maxton moved close. “I am sorry. Please know that.”

“Oh, I do, Cal.” Miranda Bormann’s voice softened seconds before the hard light returned to her eyes. “I’m afraid it’s not me you have to convince though. There’s the family and I do believe several laws were broken.”

“You can’t do this!” Maxton cried, all trace of apology and humbleness gone.

“Actually, she can,” Paula interjected.

"She's the DA, in case you didn't know." Miranda Bormann smiled. "I'd believe her if I were you."

"Are you really going to make a bigger deal over this than we have to?" Hayden Bormann looked just as outraged as Maxton.

"You made it a *bigger deal* when you stole from me and then involved your cousin to help you hide it."

"Oh to hell with you, *Aunty*!" Hayden Bormann lashed out, shaking off the restraining hand his cousin set to his shoulder. "You talk about stealing when you and Uncle Hank had more than you were entitled to! Uncle Hank hoarded everything because he was the firstborn."

Miranda Bormann rolled her eyes. "That's not true. Everyone was well looked after in your grandparents' wills."

"And Henry best of all." Hayden sneered. "He took over half my dad's inheritance."

"Because your father was unfit to care for it back then!" Miranda Bormann raged. "How long was it before his get-richer-quicker schemes cost him everything? You and your mother would've been homeless were it not for your uncle. His stepping in made your father a better man in the end."

"Oh yes! We mustn't forget to grovel at the feet of my uncle—the great Henry Bormann! I want what's rightfully mine!"

Amid Hayden Bormann's rant, Paula noticed Linus. His expression radiated a coldness anyone would've noticed were they not all riveted on the scene between Miranda Bormann and her nephews. Paula watched him look away from the family squabble, hands in his pockets.

"I think I've said all I should." Hayden Bormann managed to look indignant in the face of his deceit. "If you want to play it this way, you can play with my lawyers."

"A fine idea, Bormann." One of the men who had remained silent spoke up finally. "Rory Crane, Detective. Philadelphia PD. My associates and I have a few questions of our own."

Maxton and Bormann stared in disbelief.

"You're arresting us?" Maxton gasped.

"Not yet," Crane said. "This might go easier for you if you cooperate from the start."

"Cooperate?" Maxton bristled and began to distance himself from his cousin. "Now wait just a damn minute! My business is on the level, always has been. Hayden came to me—"

"Cal—"

"This was his idea—"

"Cal, you lying snitch—"

"Which is it?" Paula stepped in. "Is he lying or snitching? The two kind of cancel each other out, you know?"

"What is this? Some kind of entrapment?" Hayden Bormann turned his anger on Paula. "Are you running some kind of game on my aunt—at *her* age?"

Bormann began advancing on Paula and quickly stopped in his tracks. Linus had moved from his post near the windows to intercept him. Hayden Bormann halted immediately at the sight of this evidently powerful adversary.

Paula saw that Linus wasn't stopping, however. She rushed to take his arm, before he'd covered the distance to his quarry. Tig and Eli stood as well, just as ready to hold back—or defend—their friend.

Linus didn't look at Paula but kept his gaze, then rage-darkened to a thick molasses brown, fixed on Hayden Bormann. "Crane, get this garbage out of my sight before you have to arrest me too."

The detectives wasted no time. Maxton and Bormann resumed their rants as they were led from the room. Miranda, her private investigator and his associates followed, as did Tig and Eli. Paula watched them go, knowing she should too. Yet she couldn't seem to move.

Linus had returned to his spot by the window. "You should go," he told her. "Don't worry, Paula. I'm good."

"I know, I—" She sighed, then turned, allowing a sudden sense of defeat to consume her. "Bye, Linus." She didn't wait for him to return the farewell, knowing that would have broken her heart into a million more shards. She sprinted for the door and left without further delay.

Philadelphia had become an increasingly frigid terrain. Still, the brutal chill did nothing to discourage Paula's guests from turning out in force. That evening, she entertained from the home she kept in the quiet elegance of Chestnut Hill, one of Philadelphia's most desired communities. The invitation said she was celebrating the next chapter in her life, but offered no further clues. Paula didn't keep her guests in suspense too long and made the announcement that she wouldn't be seeking reelection to the DA's office.

The guests didn't seem as surprised as their hostess expected. Paula was the one surprised, in fact, when the majority of the people in the room chose not to believe her. At any rate, the night was off to a fantastic start, made more festive when the deputy mayor encouraged his fellow partygoers to place their bets on whether or not the DA would follow through on her plans.

"I, for one, am glad to hear you're pushing back from work. That way your calendar will be free when you get my invite." Rayelle tried to keep her expression schooled when she shared the tidbit later that evening.

Intrigue had Paula lifting an eyebrow. "Invite? To what?" she asked.

Rayelle cast a quick look over her shoulder. "Eli's ready to pop the question to Clarissa."

Paula's light eyes widened. "Seriously?" Her voice was hushed.

Rayelle replied with a smug nod and then looked a smidge concerned. "Keep it to yourself, alright? It's still in the planning stages."

"Got it." Paula sighed. "I should tell you, Ray, I don't know how in the mood I am for another Bahamas getaway."

"Good, since this won't be one. My girl Clari is more of a snow fan."

"That's right." Paula winced, recalling that Clarissa

David had grown up in the sun. "Well, keep me posted. Especially on the guest list."

It was Rayelle's turn to wince. "Things still complicated with you and Linus?"

"Complicated." Paula smiled in confirmation.

"So is he coming tonight?"

"Doubtful." Paula shook her head to ward off impending tears. "A lot of what happened with Miranda Bormann and her nephew reminds him of his past family stuff. I think he's too focused on whatever that did to him to focus on what's happening between us right now."

"What are you gonna do?"

"Only thing I can do." Paula shrugged. "I'll fight it."

Rayelle smiled and nodded her approval.

"And you?" Paula's smile was a sly one when her new friend seemed confused. "I hope you don't think you and Barker were inconspicuous. When you were in the room, he could barely stop looking at you."

Rayelle gave her own lazy shrug. "Well, that's how it was arranged, right? All of us being coupled off."

"And that's all?"

Ray rolled her eyes. "Well, hell no, Paula. I mean, have you seen him? He's gorgeous." She shook off the admission and suddenly appeared a little woeful. "Gorgeous and smart and accomplished and comes from money and…so not for me. Mine is not the kind of background to be considered the proper sort for a guy whose family money dates back to before the Civil War."

Paula inclined her head in acknowledgment of the

well-known pedigree of Philadelphia's most respected reporter.

"You know, Ray, all of what you're saying? It's pretty much the same thing I told myself about Linus."

"I know, but you're the DA, Paula, and a lawyer before that." Ray cast an uncertain look around the large, warmly festive room. "I manage a night club and we both know what I did before that."

"Honey, Barker doesn't care about that."

"No. Not now he doesn't, but he would eventually."

Paula arched a brow. "Sounds like you'll be keeping your eye on the guest list for our next trip too."

Ray sighed out her laughter. "Are we a pair or what?"

Paula moved close and bumped her shoulder to Ray's. "Doubtful on that. I *know* what I want, but it sounds like you still need convincing. Just don't stress it so much, alright?" She let her expression turn coy. "I'm pretty sure you'll have a good time being convinced." She gave Ray another nudge and headed off.

Paula made her way hastily through the crowd then, only allowing herself to get tangled in the briefest of conversations. She'd meant what she had said to Ray. She knew what she wanted. She knew, and she was going after it. As it wouldn't do for the DA to be caught sneaking out of her own party, she made her way around to the kitchen and into the short corridor off the pantry. The caterers were all cordoned off to the opposite side of the large area nearest the dining room. In no danger of being discovered, she bundled up for the weather and set out. She gave one last glance over her shoulder and then turned back into the night and right into Linus.

His smile flashed brilliant white as he grinned. “Doesn’t say much for the party when it’s being ditched by the hostess.”

“I’ll have you know I throw amazing parties.” Paula gave a saucy toss of her head, her tone one of playful indignation.

“Mmm…but not amazing enough to keep you on the premises, huh?”

She sobered a bit then. “I had something to handle.”

“More amazing than your party?”

Emotion had her clearing her throat. “I’m hoping it’ll turn out to be.”

“Can you spare me a few minutes before you leave?” he asked.

“I can spare you more than that. It’s you I was coming to see.”

Linus sobered then too. “I see.”

“I don’t think you do, L. I’m not giving up. I know Miranda Bormann’s revelations threw us for a loop, but that’s finished now. I won’t give up on finding out what happened—*all* of what happened—that night to change you. To find out what put the sadness in your eyes and the anger in your heart.” She squeezed her eyes shut, then opened them quick to reveal the defiance lurking.

“I know you never want to share it and that’s just too damn bad. I don’t care if you hate my questions—I love you and I won’t lose you again. I can’t let you keep carrying the weight of the past on your own.”

Linus seemed to absorb her words and then gave an

obedient nod. "I get it, Paula. Um, do you think I could come in now?"

Paula finally realized how biting the wind was as it seeped beneath the hem of her coat. It assaulted the thin legs of her pantsuit with icy daggers. Tugging the cuff of his jacket, she brought him in from the night.

"This way." She directed him along a back staircase. The second floor corridor was lit by the soft gold of electric candles.

The first door they approached was partly opened. The unmistakable flicker of firelight danced against it. Linus smiled, pushing the door farther open as the delectable aroma of apples and spices filled his nostrils.

"Already smells like Christmas in here," he said.

"I like to get a jump on the holidays."

"Speaking of being jumped, where's your security? I expected them when I decided to take the back way in. What's up? Do you leave them behind when you trade your penthouse for the quiet life?"

"They're around. Just not on heightened alert."

Linus's chocolate browns narrowed. "Maybe they should be, with you sneaking out into the night by yourself."

"It was to see you."

"A worthy cause—don't get me wrong—but safety first, P. I'm pretty sure you've got your share of enemies. This Bormann thing certainly helped you add to 'em."

Paula rolled her eyes. "Keeps the job exciting."

"And where do things stand with that? With the Bormanns?"

"Better than I'd have guessed considering the initial

evidence, but it turns out that Hayden Bormann wasn't as careful as he claimed."

"He left a trail." Linus watched Paula nod to confirm his guess.

"His close-as-a-brother cousin is ready to turn on him in hopes of saving his own business," she added. "Looks like the Bahamas project wasn't their first job together."

Linus nodded over the developments. "Keep me posted, okay?"

"I promise."

Silence settled into the cozy den. Muffled music, laughter and conversation gently radiated through the floor and added to the relaxing aura that seemed to permeate the space.

Linus shrugged out of his jacket. "Have a seat, Paula," he urged.

Paula removed her coat and, seeing Linus's reaction, waited. His dark gaze scanned the chic jumpsuit—a black number with silver piping.

"That your, uh, usual hostess attire?" he asked.

"When I entertain out here, which I rarely do."

"Glad to hear it."

Surprised by the surge of self-consciousness instilled by his words, Paula crossed her arms over her chest. The suit's V-cut bodice gave an onlooker a modest, albeit enticing, view. Paula decided to walk the room, but Linus stopped the move. Pulling at her arms, he slid his own around her waist and tugged her near as his head dipped. He took her mouth with a strong thrust that she instantly reciprocated. Greedy to have him closer, her arms circled his neck, and she stood on the toes of her icepick pumps to more accurately align her body with his.

Hungrily, Paula pushed her tongue against his, moaning feverishly when he broke the kiss. He devoured the supple honey-toned flesh of her neck, his tongue leaving a warm, wet trail to her clavicle. He took her off her feet in order to suckle the spot from a more satisfying angle.

Paula's hands were busy at the dark wool jacket he wore over a gray shirt open at the collar and hanging outside his dark trousers. Linus rested his forehead against the crook of her neck and stole several seconds to settle his breathing. Then, before she knew it, he was putting Paula to her feet and retreating.

"Baby, you need to listen to me now, okay?"

Paula nodded, blinking obsessively as if to dash away the arousal that all but screamed inside her. "Right," she said. "Sorry."

Linus replied with a crooked smile. "Nothing to apologize for, remember? None of this was about you. I can't even blame my brother. Lantz…he wasn't doing anything different from his usual—taking advantage of the situation. He thought getting together for drinks and reminiscing over our grandmother on her birthday would soften me up enough to share the wealth. I told myself not to go. The fact that he tracked me down there with you told me this was going to be a situation best avoided but…well… I hadn't seen him in years and he, um, he's my brother."

Linus lent Paula a tired smile then that quickly turned into a grimace. "'Course it was everything I expected—started off well, got ugly halfway through. When I said no to his needing $100K to back a deal he wanted into, he started going on about how he wanted what was his. Then he blamed our grandmother for keeping him down, for not letting him be who he was."

Linus grimaced. "When I stood up for her," he continued, "and reminded him of all the money he'd already lost on his schemes and how she had just been trying to protect him, he said she had just been trying to control him—keep him under her thumb. He said she'd wanted him to behave the way she wanted. 'Not me, Line, not me,' that's what he said. He left and I haven't seen or heard from him since. When I got back to the room that night I—" He paused, pacing the room then like a caged tiger while he smoothed both hands over his head.

"I kept thinking about what he said…about our grandmother wanting us to behave the way *she* dictated, and I realized he was right."

Paula went to him then. "Linus—"

"Wait." His voice held a pleading tone. "Wait and hear me, okay?"

She hesitated, but eventually gave the nod he wanted.

"I behaved, and I got what was mine. All the years Lantz rebelled, pouring hundreds of thousands down the drain, throwing the most horrific tantrums 'til she gave in and gave him the money. He'd steal it when she wouldn't."

He grinned, shook his head. "We'd have the worst fights over the way he treated her—arguments really. But when I got to the point where I just flat out wanted to kick his ass, she held me back. She said Lantz was just finding his way—told me to be patient with him. She let his ways slide, asked me to go along with it and I did, even—even when I knew there was no changing him. Still I went along, stifled my anger and never let myself dwell on the fact that Lantz was free to let *his ways* run riot while I had to restrain mine until—"

"You exploded." Paula's interruption was quiet.

Linus came to take her hand then. Squeezing, he eased her back to sit on the loveseat.

"I had tried to find you when I got back, before I… where were you?"

"You had gotten me that time in the spa, remember? You'd told me unexpected business had come up and that was your way of apologizing."

"Right." Linus smiled over the memory. "I bummed around the room for twenty minutes or so before I lost it. Funny thing is, what broke me wasn't anger over Lantz—it was my gran. She took us in, put her life on hold to do it. Nobody could've raised us better and I—I was angry at *her*."

He leaned over, hands going to his head again. "That I could really feel that way, it made me feel like I was no better than Lantz was, and I, um, there was nothing I could do but give in to it."

"But you were just a kid when all that happened." Paula scooted close to squeeze his hand. "Dealing with it when you became a man was the only choice you had."

"Dealing with it has never made me feel like a man, but like a kid—a weak kid." His voice was like stone. "Giving myself over to the rage, it felt so good,

Paula. Like—like a weight was off." He grunted an ill-humored laugh. "Didn't take me long to see that it was killing me. I couldn't have been with you while I was going through all that, Paula—you wouldn't have understood it. Hell…*I* didn't understand it. I finally mastered the rage, though…thought I was done with it too until I tried to talk to you about it. Hmph. Didn't take me long to see what a grip it still had over me."

"Linus." Paula took both his hands then, squeezing them hard inside hers. "Struggling to shake this doesn't make you weak. It makes you human." She squeezed his hands harder still.

"Not wanting to be with me while you're going through this," she added with a regretful shake of her head, "well, that just makes you stupid."

Linus grinned, though a sober element lingered in his eyes. "Whether it makes me weak, human or stupid, I never want you to see me like that again. It's clear that I can't promise you those memories don't still carry weight with me."

"That's not a promise you should make anyway, and the fact that you can't make it isn't good enough reason for us to be apart," Paula decided and scooted even closer.

Linus's smile was proof of his approval. "I agree, Madam DA," he said, putting her on his lap to satisfy his need to have her closer still. He cupped her chin. "I love you."

"I love you." She gave his words back to him and set her forehead against his.

"I guess the only way to keep those memories

weighted down is to put new ones on top of them," he said.

"Better ones," Paula countered.

"Ones we'll never want to forget. I'll spend every day making good on that, Paula."

"Every day," she emphasized.

"Every day you'll have me."

"There was a time I thought I'd have you every day for the rest of my life." Paula blinked against the sudden pressure of tears—but they were happy ones.

"There was a time I thought that too. I still do. Will you have me, Paula?"

Instead of a verbal reply, Paula kissed him. Linus's response embodied and signified the love, desire and promise they at last felt free to explore.

"Every day, Paula?" Linus insisted on his answer.

She cupped his face and squeezed. "Every day, Linus. Every day."

* * * * *